TYRANNY
of the
FEY

Terry Bartley

Book Formatting by Derek Murphy @Creativindie

Tyranny of the Fey

For information contact :
Starlight King Press
http://www.starlightkingpress.com

Book and Cover design by Deryl Arrazaq
Map by Sekcer
ISBN: 979-8-9877958-2-8

Second Edition: November 2023

10 8 6 4 2 1 3 5 7 9

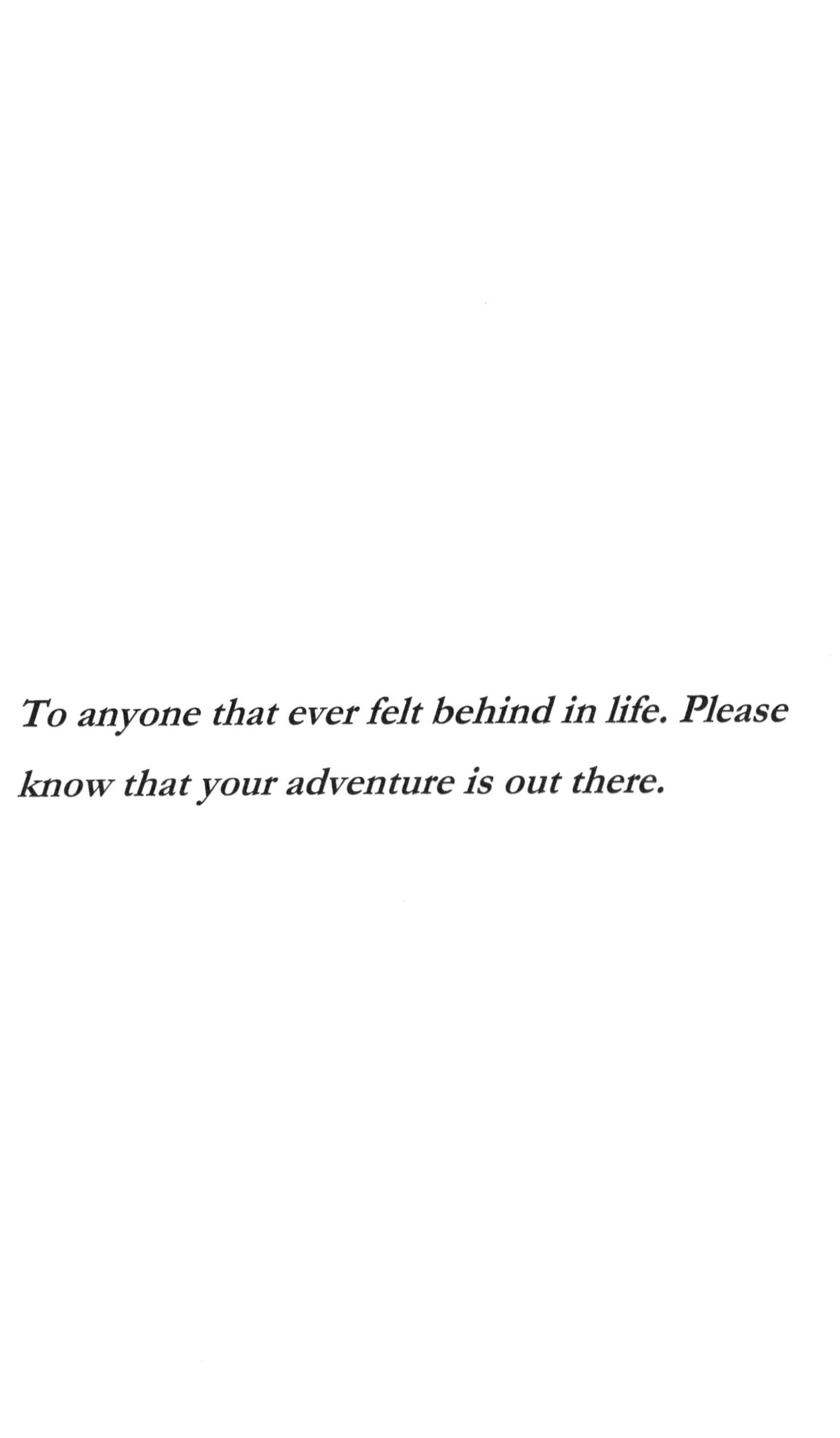

To anyone that ever felt behind in life. Please know that your adventure is out there.

Galevyn
N
Jungle of Despair
Arcana University
Anglac
Valnan
Ferreira
Ronan
Montläken
Éindi Gra
Reyes
Manos

Bultine
Daragon
Yokuatsu
Gajog
Tag
Kapoor
Dhanri

CONTENTS

Rowena Zarin

A Letter Concerning the Magical Energy Crisis

My name is Dr. Rowena Zarin, and I am worried about our home. Elven society is completely built on magic. Our water and temperature control comes from elemental magic. Our public transportation system is dependent on spatial magic. Our entertainment industry heavily relies on illusion magic. All of this could be threatened by the loss of magical energy.

Magical energy is self-renewing; every authority on magical research can agree on this. However, it does not renew at the same speed that we are consuming it. Our population is growing and our dependence on magic continues to increase, just as the Elven Empire should as the inter-realm industrial leader. However, if we continue without exploring other solutions, the problem will only worsen. Magical researchers, such as myself, are actively working on ways to reduce the consumption of magical energy. I have seen elves at every class level embrace my new development that replaces the elemental magic used in most cooking devices with a permanent portal to the Fire Realm. These devices reducemagic consumption by only requiring a small amount to widen or limit the size of the portal. However, these small fixes are not enough.

Wallace Ashiere has argued that this problem isn't as serious as everyone in the magical research community claims. He has said that magic ebbs and flows and that it is simply on a downswing at the moment. Ashiere would have you all believe that we can continue to live the way that we are living and that our magical energy will never run out. With all due respect to Mr. Ashiere, that is a pedestrian way to look at things. He does not have the credentials or the experience that those of us that have studied magic for centuries have developed. It is not a question of opinion, as he claims. It is a question of experience. Mr. Ashiere simply has not presented sufficient nor convincing evidence that the magical energy of the Fey Realm can withstand our extensive use of it. Our society needs to understand that whenever someone of Mr. Ashiere's credentials claims to be an authority, all they are capable of doing is stating an impassioned opinion. Asking someone like Mr. Ashiere for his thoughts on matters of magical research is like asking a house Gnome or field Pixies to purchase land. I feel like we can all agree it best that we keep civilians pursuing traditional civilian careers and for the minor fey on the menial tasks best suited for them, so that Elves are free for better uses of their time.

No, we cannot take the views of Mr. Ashiere, or those like him, seriously if we intend to thrive as a leading nation. Something must be done to address this problem, but what can we do that can actually make a difference? I have done extensive research, and after much trial and error, I believe I have stumbled upon the answer. I believe the answer lies in other outside-the-box solutions using spatial magic. While our realm struggles to produce enough magical energy to keep up with the demand of our kingdom, there is another realm out there that contains ample magical energy that we could pull from for our needs, just as we use heat from the Fire Realm. We could essentially "mine" magical energy from this new realm.

I saw such lush plant life when I gazed through the portal into this realm. It would put the Duchy of Spring to shame. This plant life thrives because of the incredibly rich elemental magic that flows throughout this realm. However, this realm is not only rich in elemental magic, I have personally confirmed that this realm is also capable of spatial, divination, charm, illusion, and transmutation magic. Beyond this, my initial experiments have led me to believe that this realm contains disciplines of magic that Elvenkind has yet to discover. The potential of this realm cannot be ignored.

While I have conducted some initial research on this realm, fully exploring an entirely undiscovered realm is not something I am able to undertake alone. I have seen evidence that this realm is home to some sort of indigenous population, and I do not know if they are friendly or even capable of sentient thought. I am writing to the Queen of Summer and the Queen of Winter in order to request a full team of official researchers to join me in an expedition into this realm. It is my opinion that the future of the Elven race lies in this new realm. Let us explore it together.

Sincerely,

Dr. Rowena Zarin

A Letter Concerning the Material Realm

To Captain Blythe Ferdinand:

I was very pleased upon learning that the Queens of Summer and Winter accepted my proposal to further explore this new realm as a way to subsidize the magical energy of the Fey Realm. Their response advised that the majority of our funds would be coming with the military contingent that would be joining us on the expedition and that you would be my contact with the royal government moving forward. However, they did mention that some of the funds would be reimbursable if I needed to prepare anything before your arrival.

As it stands, my excitement at deepening our understanding exceeds my scientific logic, and I have led a small contingent of researchers into the realm. I utilized spatial magic to open up a portal just large enough for our group. Thus, we have set up a small encampment in the jungle I had mentioned in my previous missive. Though small, I do believe this headquarters should be large enough to house my researchers and the modest military unit that you will be leading here. My assistants and I were able to tap into this realm's elemental magic to construct structures that would functionally work for our purposes without disrupting the local ecosystem.

I was quite impressed at the functionality of the elemental magic here. I have used elemental magic to construct horticulture from natural resources in the fey realm, but nothing this elaborate. The variety and quantity of fauna in this realm is truly a marvel, and the essence of its elemental magic complements it perfectly.

I look forward to showing you the research labs and dorm units we were able to construct by encouraging the trees and bushes to grow how we needed them. My mind currently races at the other uses we may be able to find for the magic of this realm.

This letter is to serve as an update brief on what my team and I have uncovered during our time in this unexplored world. I wish to keep you as current as possible so that you may best utilize both of our times upon our initial meeting.

First things first, my team and I decided that this place needed a name. Continuing to refer to it as "the new realm" became cumbersome quickly. Due to the tangible nature of everything in this realm, especially when comparing it to our Fey Realm, we decided to call this the "Material Realm." That is how I will be referring to it moving forward.

About a day into our studies, a group of natives discovered our encampment. They approached us more with curiosity than hostility. I used a basic translation spell to communicate with them. It turns out they are part of a population of sub-elf species. One such species refers to itself as "Human." These Humans have small rounded ears and are less lithe than an average Elf. They seem to have more body mass and larger fat deposits distributed throughout their body. This likely developed evolutionarily from their need to hunt down their own food. These deposits of fat allow them to live for multiple days without sustenance, if needed. Of course, we Elves have never had this problem as Fey food has much more concentrated nutrition, requiring less to sustain our bodies. Humans have hair on their heads and faces, as Elves do, yet I was surprised to see that some of them had hair growing out of their chests and all over their arms and legs. I suppose this was also an evolutionary adaptation to what I presume are colder periods in the Material Realm. Finally, the skin tone of these Humans seems to be darker than that of a High Elf, yet lighter than that of a River Elf.

Additionally, there is a species that refers to itself as "Orcs." Orcs are much larger than humans or Elves. They have much more in the way of muscle mass, yet they do still carry a good bit of fat content. Not only are they taller, but they are also much broader than an Elf or Human. While the humans have voices in a similar tone to elves, orcs have much deeper voices, with a bit of a growl present in any word they spoke. Orcs also have hair throughout their body, in similar places to humans. Their skin tones, however, were more earthy. The orcs I have met have skin tones of gray, brown, and green.

We learned that the orcs and the humans live side-by-side in this jungle. They have learned to work together. For example, the hunting party we met was composed of humans and orcs. The orcs tended to confront the larger prey, while the humans used crude ranged weapons to shoot down smaller prey. Once on our short travels with them, the humans would even attack larger prey with ranged weaponry while the orcs confronted them physically. I was impressed at how this primitive culture has adapted to find an efficient way to survive. Notably, the orcs and humans see each other as equals. This was a startling contrast to how we Elves have viewed the Fey sub-races. How bizarre, to imagine elves living alongside Pixies, Gnomes, or Trolls in a similar fashions. Our history has taught us that society can only function when the superior race institutes a strict caste system to maintain order. I have considered if, in the coming centuries, as the society in the Material Realm develops, will the brighter humans overtake the orcs, or if the stronger orcs will dominate the humans. With any luck, a comprehensive sociological study can be conducted in the Material Realm. That would be very interesting to read after I've reached my third century.

Once this hunting party assessed that my team and I posed no immediate threat to them, they invited us back to their camp to meet their leader. Upon our arrival, it became clear that the native population had not developed ways to utilize the full functionality of the Material Realm's magic. They lived in primitive huts constructed from dried wood harvested from the jungle, lashed with dried grasses and vines. While the ingenuity was commendable, I couldn't help but feel sad that they have been forced to live in such conditions. Perhaps, upon your consultation, my team and I may teach these people some basic spells to help them live more comfortably.

When we met their chief, I was able to witness something incredible. The hunting party addressed their chief and immediately bowed in front of him. He then waved basic ritual implements, such as color sticks and gemstones, while chanting an incantation. I do not know if he was fully aware he was channeling magic. As he completed the ritual, all the wounds sustained during their hunting expedition were healed in front of our eyes. Bruises lightened until they faded into their natural skin tones, cuts knitted themselves back together, and broken bones snapped back into place. In all of my time as a magical researcher, I had never seen anything like this. I have decided to call this discipline of magic "healing."

The sheer possibilities of this new type of healing magic could be revolutionary for our people. We could cure diseases previously thought incurable.. We could assist the sub-race labor population to work longer and increase productivity. We could develop methods to save Elves that have experienced otherwise fatal injuries.

I look forward to learning ways to channel this magic, and hopefully bring some of it back to the Fey Realm. We could potentially do this through the use of localized spatial magic. I will keep you updated on our progress.

I look forward to your arrival and to any guidance you can send from the Fey Queens. If you have any need to contact me before your arrival, simply send a message to my wife. She has the means to contact me when I am traveling outside the Fey Realm.

Sincerely,

Rowena Zarin

A Letter to Address Concerns About the Material Realm Research

Spring Maiden:

I apologize for the impropriety of writing to you directly. I have come to feel like I've been backed into a corner and am running out of options. I have written the courts of your superior, the Queen of Summer, and no one there has expressed any urgency concerning my requests. I hope that a reasonable leader such as yourself may be able to understand why this matter must be addressed hastily.

As I'm sure you are aware, the Queens of Summer and Winter have recently sponsored an expedition to a new realm I have dubbed the Material Realm. I had reason to believe the realm's magic might serve as a solution to the problems facing our Kingdom. I still believe this to be true, but I believe the contingent of soldiers are approaching our research with much more force than necessary.

The Queens have sent Captain Blythe Ferdinand with a fleet of soldiers to maintain a perimeter of security around our research camp. While I found Captain Ferdinand rather short-tempered, I still thought she was reasonable. How wrong I have been!

My researchers and I had been working cooperatively with the indigenous people of the Material Realm for many weeks before Captain Ferdinand arrived. I even informed her as much in a missive I sent before her arrival. We have begun an informal partnership with the local people, who have come to accept our presence here. These people do not have the industry we built in the Fey Realm, so they must hunt for their food. We have understood this and overlooked them when their hunting parties must pass by our encampment. I informed Captain Ferdinand of this; however, it made no difference.

Captain Ferdinand ordered her soldiers to shoot down any indigenous people who approached our camp. It mattered not how many times I explained to her that they are peaceful people. She continued to fear that they could "cause trouble." I believe she dislikes the indigenous people because their ways are different from ours. She would not understand that my researchers and I had already begun to educate them so that they could better accommodate any future Elves that travel through this realm.

What happened next should be no surprise to one as intelligent and accomplished as you. An indigenous hunting party passed by our camp, and Captain Ferdinand's soldiers shot them down. They murdered a group of peaceful, innocent hunters because of a mere "feeling" Captain Blythe had about these people. These people have willingly worked with us to gain a better understanding of this world's magic. I don't disagree that if we were to continue working with these people, we would likely need to figure out some way to integrate them into our society, but they have never been an enemy to kill indiscriminately.

My concern is not just the moral failings of Captain Ferdinand. She has also impaired our research. Researching in this part of the jungle was simple because we had built a working relationship with the locals. This incident has, predictably, impaired this relationship. After I reprimanded Captain Ferdinand for her actions, I immediately met with the chief of the local settlement. The only way I could achieve even a tenuous peace was to assure the chief that I would work to lessen the militaristic element without our encampment. That is the purpose of this letter.

I have entreated the Queens of Summer and Winter to send a replacement for Captain Ferdinand and to lower the number of soldiers. They have yet to respond to my messages. I am hoping that you will personally contact them on my behalf. They may not view the concerns of a researcher as urgent, but they would listen to the Spring Maiden. I have also sent a missive to the Autumn Maiden. Perhaps the two of you can send a joint statement.

Thank you for your time. I am certain there is a solution to this problem, and we can continue the important research to save our realm. I apologize again that I have sent this to you directly, but Captain Ferdinand has forced my hand. I look forward to your timely response.

Sincerely,

Rowena Zarin, Lead Researcher

A Farewell Letter to My Loving Wife

My Beloved Dorthea,

I would like to express my deepest gratitude for the comfort you provided during my most recent visit home. The tension had grown very thick within the Material Realm Research Project, and I had believed a little time away from it would do me some good.

I regret to inform you that while I addressed my mental anguish, my absence allowed Captain Blythe Ferdinand to acquire control of the project. I am now deeply concerned that the good work I had established in this realm is undone. Captain Ferdinand's mistreatment of the indigenous population of this realm has crossed a line from which I fear there is no return.

Upon my retreat back to the Fey Realm, Captain Ferdinand commanded my researchers to determine the Material Realm's capacity for charm magic. On its face, this request did not seem unreasonable. Much of what my research team had been doing was analyzing how each known discipline of magic functioned within the Material Realm. They could not have known of Captain Ferdinand's ill intent.

Another key change to Captain Ferdinand's tactics was commanding her soldiers to capture any indigenous hunting parties instead of killing them. Again, on its face, this seems a commendable change in her indigenous policy. The wording of the order implies that Captain Ferdinand had intentions to question the hunters and release them back to their people. However, Captain Ferdinand had no intention of relinquishing these prisoners from her detainment. She instructed the researchers to suppress their free will with charm magic so that she could force them to serve the project directly.

As I returned to our research encampment, I was horrified at the blank-faced hunters that were now being seen among the soldiers and researchers. They were performing every sort of menial task, ranging from fetching tea for the researchers to digging trenches around the encampment. This project was meant to help the people of the Fey

Realm. I know that Captain Ferdinand has assured me that she is still working towards that goal; however, I must ask, at what cost?

This deep-seated feeling of guilt ruminated within my mind for days upon my return. I was technically in charge of the project, but I am no fool. I am a mere magic researcher, and Captain Ferdinand is an accomplished military leader. If I challenged her authority, she would inevitably retaliate with force. She would no doubt blame my untimely end on the indigenous people of this realm. There was already so much blood on my hands. I could not bear more evil done in my name. I knew I could no longer sit back and watch as Captain Ferdinand terrorized these people indiscriminately.

Roughly one week after returning to the project, I found myself alone in one of the research tents. I called one of these mind-controlled servants to my tent as though I had need of them. Just before I left the encampment for holiday, I had discovered a new kind of magic that had never before been studied. This realm has something I have dubbed "dispell magic." This magic is able to counter the effects of any spell, no matter the strength or permanency. I tapped into this power and released this servant from the control of Captain Ferdinand's spell. I further tapped into the divination magic to create a telepathic link so that the two of us could communicate silently.

This woman's name was Tawny, as best I could translate it into Elven. Tawny was inconsolable upon immediate release, although I did manage to calm her. She used the telepathic link to show me the horrors that Captain Ferdinand had committed, not only to the hunters, but also to the indigenous settlements themselves. Ferdinand had taken their children from their homes and sent them back to the Fey Realm. Suddenly, the future that I imagined where our people freely shared the magic of this world with those native to it was rapidly disappearing. I had welcomed pain and tragedy into this land.

I advised Tawny that there was little I could do about her fellows, but I could send her somewhere safe. She begged me to use the same technique I used to free her mind on her children, who were currently imprisoned in a large tent within the encampment. I knew it was risky, but my guilt had gotten the better of me. Saving these children may be all within my power I could do to ease the suffering of these people.

I instructed Tawny to act as my guide and to not show emotion on her face as she walked me across the encampment. She complied, and it was only a matter of minutes until we found ourselves in the company of 30 children who had been magically put to sleep. Captain Ferdinand must not have the resources to charm them yet. Tawny wanted me to free them immediately, but I knew we had to be more strategic in our rescue. I spend the next hour drawing a teleportation circle around the children. I knew my power was limited, and I had to use it wisely. The dispell magic would wake the children, but they would not be quiet; they are children. I would need to immediately teleport them after they awoke. I informed Tawny of all of this and asked her to stand inside the circle. I told her I would transport them roughly 25 miles away from this place, but she would need to take them farther from there. Captain Ferdinand will be increasing the scope of her operation, in due time.

Tawny understood and nodded at me in sullen agreement. In a quick motion I tapped into the dispell magic and released a massive pulse of its energy. No doubt, others in the encampment would become aware of it the moment it happened. Before the children stirred themselves awake, I sliced across my palm and slammed the blood into the circle. I knew that blood magic was the only way I could manage to teleport this many people.

They all disappeared, and I have since used my remaining time among the living to compose this letter. There is residual teleportation magic enough to send this to you. Once this letter is sent, I intend to confront Captain Ferdinand and attempt to retake control of this project. I have already communicated my fears to you as to the consequences of these actions. I am sending you this because these two realms need to know that there were Elves horrified by these actions. I imagine it won't be much longer until the intent of sharing this world's magic will be a distant memory. I would like to believe that the Queens of Summer and Winter would put a stop to this, if they were only made aware. However, their "lesser beings" policy has been clearly demonstrated with our realm's Gnomes and Pixiess.

Please know that I pursued this project because I believed our people could find a better way. I wanted to build a better life for you and our two children. I love the three of you with all my heart, and I wish for nothing more than to return to you. But I must do what I can to ease the suffering of these people that were so kind and helpful to me. Even though I am doing this for the indigenous people of the Material Realm, I also wish to cleanse my soul so it will not taint our children in the future. Please take care of yourself and our children.

Goodbye, My Love,

Rowena

Asha Alistar

Obedience and Opposition

"Nice moves," Aunt Poppy said. Sweat was beginning to gather on her brow. Her sandy short-cropped hair glistened in the sunlight. "You must have been practicing while I was away."

She raised her short sword to guard her face and torso and backed away from me. She certainly looked less intimidating in her formal pantsuit, but the shirt still strained from her hulking arm muscles.

"Something like that," I replied. I didn't exactly have fighting clothes, as my mother didn't approve of this hobby. But my old, beat up riding clothes worked well enough. "Or you're just getting old."

I took a deep breath and flung my head to toss my deep black ponytail around to my back. I rushed towards her and she swiped her blade in my direction. At the last moment, I dropped into a crouch and swung my leg around to trip her. She jumped before I could make contact and flipped forward, over my head. She lowered the edge of her short sword to my throat as autumn leaves fell around us.

"Got me again," I laughed as she pulled her sword away and offered me her hand. I happily took it and pulled myself up. The garden of the Autumn Maiden's estate wasn't meant for this sort of training, but it was always my favorite use of the grounds.

"You truly are getting better," she repeated.

I pushed some loose hairs behind my ear and smirked. "Still not good enough to beat you."

"Please, girl, I have been adventuring for over a century now. You are barely within your second decade," Aunt Poppy reassured.

"I just really wanted to beat you before . . . . Well, you know," I admitted.

"Asha," she began sympathetically. "Just because you're getting married doesn't mean you need to stop sparring with me."

"The future Autumn Maiden doesn't concern herself with the martial arts," I said, pointing a crooked finger at her, mimicking my grandmother. I pushed my nose out and opened my eyes a bit wider.

Aunt Poppy laughed. "You better not let her catch you doing that. That woman never forgets. You can trust me on that."

That made a chill run down my back, remembering all the times I'd been scolded by my grandmother. It's not what she says so much as how she says it. That tone will stick with you.

"But it's more than that, Aunt Poppy. I don't want sparring to just be a womanly dalliance for me. I want to be an adventurer. I want to be like you!" I meant it. The princess life never seemed to fit for me.

"I know," she said in a consolatory tone. "But sometimes we just don't get to choose our path in life."

I liked to believe she truly felt things could be different for me. Why else would she send me such detailed letters of her adventures all the time? I hoped she might know about a loophole to get me out of this.

"But you did!"

Aunt Poppy sighed. There were some things, it seemed, even great adventurers can't do. "That's the blessing of being the second born. I assure you, your father has made sacrifices because of his duty to the family. That is just something first borns get saddled with."

"It's not fair," I whined. I sounded like a small child. I always made sure to take advantage of my time with my aunt to get in all my overly dramatic complaints that I couldn't do in front of the rest of my family.

"That it is not, Asha. Life rarely is," Poppy said solemnly, turning to look towards the Autumn Maiden's expansive manor house.

"It's just," I began, "The way you talk about the material realm makes it sound like there is so much more opportunity there."

"It is that," Aunt Poppy admitted. "But there are troubles there, too. I'll be heading back there after tonight's dinner. Perhaps if you make a good impression your grandmother might let you tag along."

I smiled at the thought, even though I knew it was a far-fetched fantasy.

"Asha! Sister! It is almost time!" My sister Tinsley called, rushing from the large decorative glass double doors on the back of the manor house.

"Very well, Tinsley," I relented and began following behind her.

"Eh, not so fast," Aunt Poppy said.

I looked down and noticed the training sword still in my hand. I handed it over.

"I get it," Aunt Poppy began, "I've had more than a few first dates I'd wished I'd brought a weapon along, but it may not offer a good first impression."

"Probably not," I laughed.

"Hurry up, Asha!" Tinsley protested, looking back. She had already gotten prepared for the dinner with a lace-trimmed flowy yellow dress. Her black hair was tied up in an elaborate braid. "Lord Kingsley could be here any minute!"

"Tinsley," I said, running to catch up to her. "The letter said that Lord Kingsley would arrive at sundown. We have nearly two hours left."

"Yes, but he could be early. Just imagine if he comes early and you're still dirty from sparring. What must he think of our family," Tinsley worried, wringing her hands.

"Dear sister," I said, stepping in front of her. "Then surely he must know if he inconveniences us by coming early, it is my prerogative to make him wait."

I booped her nose and skipped ahead, pushing through the door to our family sitting room. I was greeted with solemn faces from my mother and grandmother.

"Take those dirty boots off this instant!" My grandmother, Arabella Alistar, screamed at me. I quickly complied and stood at near attention.

I don't know if she had already prepared for the dinner or not, as she is always dressed formally. Even though we are in our private home, she always says that the Autumn Maiden must be ready to take guests at a moment's notice. This afternoon, she was wearing a deep maroon gown with leaves embroidered around the trim. It was always leaves with her. Her gray hair was plaited in her signature three-strand braid.

"Honestly, Asha, do you have any idea how hard your mother and I have worked to ensure this house is perfect for your future husband?" Grandmother scolded .

I could see my mother, Priya Mehmet Alistar, roll her deep brown eyes behind my grandmother's back. We all knew my mother had really done all the cleaning. My grandmother had only bossed her around and found fault with her choices. However, we also all knew never to question my grandmother to her face.

"Of course, Grandmother. I'm so very sorry, I wasn't thinking," I replied.

"As though that is anything new. I suppose we can't ask a leopard to change its spots, can we? Priya, dear, do you think you could do something about your daughter? Please clean her up and find something appropriate for her to wear. Surely even you can manage that," my grandmother disparaged, waving me and my mother away.

My mother stood up and crossed the room to ascend the stairs. I lowered my head and quickly followed behind, hoping to avoid notice. I wasn't so lucky.

"Posture, Asha!" my grandmother yelled, "You are going to develop a hunched back!"

"Yes, Grandmother," I said sheepishly, straightening.

As we reached the upstairs hallway, I strapped myself in for the guilt trip I knew my mother was about to take me on.

"Asha Anvi Alistar." my mother almost always begans these speeches with my full name. "How can you be so careless? Don't you realize the sacrifices I've made for you? When I left Kapoor and transported my life to the Fey Realm, I left everyone I loved behind. Do you have any idea how hard that was for me?"

"I feel like I have some idea, but I'm sure you'll tell me again," I joked, trying to lighten the mood.

"This is all some joke to you, isn't it? I don't think you realize how hard life is in the Material Plane. People like us are persecuted there. The people there hate Elves," she explained.

"Mom, people hate us here! We are basically the only people in the Fey Realm with dark skin. People look at us like we are some kind of alien, which I guess, we kind of are," I argued.

"Which is why it was so incredible that your father chose to marry me. He took a risk that has the potential to elevate River Elves to levels unseen in centuries. But that can only happen if our family can move through their social customs."

"I know that, Mom, but what about our customs? I don't even know all the names of our people's holidays."

"I know this is hard for you to understand, but the great hope of the River Elves rests on your shoulders. We can't make any mistakes. You can't make any mistakes. Please, listen to what I'm saying, I'm begging you," my mother pleaded.

"Very well, Mother," I said, code switching back to the High Elven woman my mother wanted me to be. It often felt like the only person that saw me for me was my Aunt Poppy. It gets exhausting pretending to be someone else.

"That's good, Asha," my mother said. "Let's clean you up and make you look like a woman this Lord Kingsley will want to marry."

"Yes, Mother," I relented. This wasn't an argument I was going to win.

My mother instructed me to undress while she prepared a hot bath for me. As I stood naked and alone in my bedchambers, I couldn't help but notice all the ways I could escape this place. I didn't have anything resembling a plan, but the thought of "away," sounded very appealing. The large window in my room led to a rose garden below, just one story down. I could easily fashion a rope out of my opulent sheets and scurry my way down before my mother returned. There were no windows on the lower level directly below this room, so it wouldn't be hard to avoid detection. I'd be free to chase the life of adventure I'd always dreamed of. Though, I suppose, the gardening staff may spot me and tell my family.

There's also the secret passage behind my wardrobe that leads to a dank chamber below the Autumn Manor. It is ancient and likely used by earlier generations to sneak out. It made me wonder what sort of trouble my grandmother could have possibly gotten into in her youth. That wouldn't work, though; the servants now use those walkways to travel unnoticed throughout the manor. Surely I would be recognized.

I also briefly considered the washroom that I shared with my sister, Tinsley. Tinsley was certainly downstairs with our grandmother and I could likely sneak out of there and find a way out through the back entrance of the manor. But again, surely someone would catch me. There were likely servants using fire magic there to warm up my bath as I stood here.

Before I could earnestly consider an escape plan, my mother returned with a large, poofy, bright orange dress. There were leaf accents stitched along each seam, and garish, brightly colored apples and oranges generously placed along the lengthy skirt. I'm certain many girls would find it beautiful. I found it excessive.

"What are you doing just standing in your room in the nude?" My mother chastised. "Get yourself into the bath. I see that I'm going to have to hold your hand through every part of this if I expect it to go well."

I nodded and walked into the washroom. As promised, my mother followed, guided me into the tub, and started scrubbing my body. To this day, I can think of no act more mortifying than being an able-bodied woman, 23 years of age, while your mother bathes you like a child. I still have nightmares about it.

After my bath, my mother dressed me in the ridiculous dress she'd brought, curled my hair into luscious waves, and finished the look with a wreath of Autumn flowers atop my head. I'm sure I was the perfect image of future royalty.

By this time, I could see the sun beginning to set. My entire family had already gathered outside, awaiting Lord Kingsley's carriage. My mother and I walked out to join them. Just as we'd joined our family, as if on cue, a pair of alaricorns began drifting slowly into our front garden. They were beautiful, with perfectly white manes and broad, angelic wings. Their horns shone like the finest silver and occasionally produced a subtle spark. Behind them, an elegant carriage was attached. It had gold accents and more in-laid aquamarine gemstones than were aesthetically pleasing. Aquamarine is the official gemstone of the Windsor family and I suppose Lord Kingsley's family didn't want us thinking it was just some commoner's carriage pulled by two of the rarest steeds in all of the Fey Realm.

My five-year-old brother, Brigsby, was immediately enamored with the creatures.

"Those unicorns have wings!" He exclaimed to my father, the Crown Prince of Autumn, Sterling Alistar.

"They do!" He agreed. My father always understood that there was no need to ruin the fun of children with semantics.

"Can I pet them?" Brigsby asked.

"We'll have to ask Lord Kingsley," my father informed. "Do you think you can wait a few moments until we introduce ourselves?"

"Yes, I can do it!" Brigsby assured him.

I smiled at his youthful zeal.

As the carriage settled, the doors magically swung open, and Lord Kingsley stepped out. He was very handsome, in an objective sense. A tall elven man with a strong jawline. He had short, but flowing, locks of dark brown hair. His face was cleanly shaven and completely devoid of expression. I've never understood why rich people think showing no emotion makes them more attractive. And in my experience, this isn't just an Elven thing, all types of rich people think that emotion makes them ugly. To me, it makes them look bored. Knowing my young self, I'm certain I shared the same look, but only because I actually was bored. He approached my grandmother first.

"It is such an honor to meet the exalted Autumn Maiden," Lord Kingsley said as he bowed deeply.

"You may rise. We are pleased your family has elected for you to join us this evening. We hope you will enjoy the dinner we have prepared for you," my grandmother concluded, leading us into the dining hall.

"A meal prepared by the Autumn Maiden herself must be incredible," Lord Kingsley said, knowing full well that a woman of my grandmother's stature would never sully herself by preparing her own food.

My grandmother blushed and said, "The gentleman flatters."

We all lined up at the front of the dining hall as my grandmother took her seat at the head of the table.

"Asha Alistar, allow me to introduce you to Lord Kingsley Windsor, your betrothed," my grandmother said, gesturing for us to greet each other.

I wanted to make a quip about how I was with her outside when he introduced himself, but I'd already gotten myself into enough trouble. Instead, I simply said, "A pleasure," and offered him my hand.

He kissed it. "The pleasure is all mine. My family did not do you justice. They told me you were beautiful, but they didn't tell me you were stunning."

He was really going all out with these compliments. I giggled despite my disdain to avoid retching right there on the fine carpeting and retreated to my seat beside my grandmother. He claimed his seat opposite me. And so it went, with my grandmother giving each of my family permission to sit. Next my parents, then my aunt, then finally my siblings. For once, I missed sitting with the children. At least they would be permitted to have an enjoyable conversation.

As we began eating our first course, the conversation went about as you'd expect. We spoke nothing of substance and basically kept repeating the same two or three greetings to one another. My grandmother was too intimidating for Lord Kingsley to show any vulnerability in front of, so we just talked about nothing. I grew tired of it by my third butternut squash crostini.

I excused myself and snuck into the sitting room. It was less for the leaf patterned velvet sofas and more for the lack of immediate visual reminders of what was to come. I began pacing back and forth and considered what kind of life I would have with Lord Kingsley. One thing was for sure, it would be extraordinarily ordinary. That wasn't the life I wanted for myself. I wanted adventure, I wanted excitement, and that tall glass of Elven milk was not capable of providing that for me.

"Lady Asha." I heard a male voice call from the side hallway.

I turned around and saw Lord White Bread himself.

"Hello, Lord Kingsley. I'm sorry to keep you waiting," I apologized.

"No, no trouble," he assured. "I just wanted to see if what was bothering you is the same thing that is bothering me."

This was intriguing.

"Which is?" I inquired.

"I hate these arranged marriage play act things we have to do. I hate the idea of an arranged marriage. My parents did it, and they seem happy, but I just don't know," Lord Kingsley confided.

It was nice to know that I wasn't the only noble that felt frustrated with the expectation to do things just because it was what everyone had always done. Maybe we didn't have to do this. We wouldn't be the first to stray from tradition.

"My parents didn't have an arranged marriage," I confessed with a smile.

"Really?" he said with a smirk. "The Autumn Maiden's son married a woman of his choosing?"

"Turns out, this part of the Fey realm doesn't typically have people with brown skin," I remarked.

"I had noticed that," he joked.

"I'm sorry, I don't want this life," I admitted. "I want a life of adventure, and being the future Autumn Maiden doesn't offer that to me."

"You know you'd be giving up your position as heir of one of the number two ruling families in the Fey realm?" he asked.

"I do, in fact," I said. "I just don't see the appeal of mediating feuds between noble families, and doing whatever the Winter Queen tells me to do."

"It does not sound like adventure, I will admit that," Lord Kingsley said.

"I don't know what to do," I said. "I don't want to trap you into this life if you don't want it."

"Oh, I want it," Lord Kingsley said, "The power and security is appealing to me. But I don't want you to feel obligated to provide that to me."

"Really?" I asked.

"Yes. You should go. Take one of my alaricorns out front, and give her this." He placed a small green berry in my hand.

"What is it?" I asked.

"That is a sacred berry of the Spring Court, called a Wanta. My family raises them. When fed to an alaricorn, they transport themselves and their rider to the Material Plane," he explained.

"Why do you think I want to go to the Material Plane?" I asked.

"Because if you run, nowhere in the Fey Realm will be safe for you. If you want adventure, that is where you'll have to go," he said.

"You're not wrong," I agreed. "How can I repay you?"

"Live the life you want," he said, "That's what I'm going to try to do."

"Thank you," I said, then I leaned in and kissed him on the lips gently. As far as first kisses go, this one certainly could have been worse.

"You're welcome, Asha Alistar," Lord Kingsley said.

"Goodbye," I said, walking quietly outside. The sensible part of me wanted to go upstairs and pack, but the adventurous part of me had waited too long for an opportunity like this.

As I passed through the door, I spotted my sheathed training sword leaning against the outside wall attached to a belt. I picked it up and strapped the belt around my dress.

I proceeded to approach one of the alaricorns and reached to scratch its nose. It lowered its head and happily complied. I walked around, released the carriage hitch, and mounted the alaricorn. I stroked its mane heartily and reached around to feed it the berry. As I sat astride the alaricorn, I watched the manor where I had spent the entirety of my life up to that point fade from view.

I didn't have time to think about how the rest of the dinner went or what my grandmother would think when she found out, because the path to adventure laid before me. And adventure waits for no one.

Out of the Fey Realm

My family home began to fade before my eyes, replaced with a bright, white light. I blinked to attempt to readjust to my new setting, but it was pointless because the light was quickly overtaken by the interior of a tavern emerging into existence around me.

I barely had time to look around whenever I heard a man yell, "You've got to be kidding me!"

The tavern looked downright dingy to me, but my only frame of reference was the homes of lords and royalty. The floor was worn, patchy hardwood, with tables and stools scattered about. There were various levels of food waste distributed about the room.

The man continued, "This is the third time this month! You wizards have to stop teleporting wherever the hell you want. Some of us are trying to run an honest business around here!"

He was a short man with a bit of a potbelly. He had short salt-and-pepper hair and pale skin. A bit of stubble was poking out of his face. Not entirely unappealing, if I'm being honest. Though, his ears did startle me. They were so short, only just level with his eyes. Not only that but they were rounded. I had never seen anything like it. He wore dark clothing and an apron, not unlike what I had seen my servants wear.

"And if you are not the most interesting man I have ever seen before!" I exclaimed at him.

His eyes narrowed in offense. "What? You are not going to come in here and just make fun of me. What is wrong with you?"

"I'm being serious, those little ears, the two-toned hair, and the way your stomach puffs out at the front and sides. You're lovely!" I explained.

"Now I know you're making fun of me. Wait, what did you say about my ears?" It was as though he had only just decided to look at me. I saw his eyes drift up to my face, and then it twisted into an expression of absolute horror. "You're an Elf! You can't be here!"

He moved towards the alaricorn tentatively and tried to shoo it out.

"I'm sorry, I don't know what you're saying. I mean, yes, I'm an Elf, but why is that a problem?" I asked. I legitimately had no idea what he was talking about.

"Are you being serious right now? You people were all over Anglachel when I was a kid, and we all know that you were enslaving the tribes to the west. There was even talk that you people were using charm magic to take advantage of the civilized people in the city. Just because you all left doesn't mean we've forgiven you." He ranted.

Obviously, I had learned in my private princess lessons that the Material Realm had been colonized by my ancestors. But for the life of me, I could not understand what he was so worked up about if all this happened back when he was a kid.

"Seriously? Can't we just let bygones be bygones? When you were a kid had to be, what, about 500 years ago?" I said, gauging his age based on the people his age I had met in the Fey Realm.

I saw his facial expression shift from confusion to curiosity to rage. "What is wrong with you!?! That's such an insane thing to say that I don't even know if it's offensive. I'm only forty years old. What kind of a person lives for 500 years?"

When I tell you I was confused, that doesn't even begin to describe it. What kind of a world had I teleported to? I knew I'd lived a sheltered life, but surely not this sheltered.

"I'm afraid I don't have the slightest idea what you're talking about," I concluded.

The man's countenance shifted back to confusion. At least now we felt the same way about the situation.

"Are you trying to tell me that you've never met a human before?" he asked.

"I'm trying to tell you that I've never even heard that word before. What did you say? Humis?" I asked. Was he talking about a kind of animal?

"HU-MAN," he pronounced exaggeratedly. "I'm talking about most of the people that live in this city."

"Please, I'm not a child. Don't talk to me like one. But I suppose, yes, you are the first of these human creatures I've met. That explains why you are so unique," I reasoned.

"I assure you, I am painfully average," he explained. "But you still can't be here. Your people still aren't exactly loved in these parts. Why are you here?"

"I'm looking for adventure," I answered sincerely. "I'm running away from an arranged marriage."

"That does sound bad," he said in a neutral tone that didn't really express sympathy. "I wish there was something I could do for you."

"Maybe there is," I said brightly. "Would you like to purchase this alaricorn?"

I would need money if I was going to live here. Selling this creature that isn't even mine seemed to make the most sense.

"Is that what that unicorn with wings is called?" he asked.

"And you thought I was ridiculous for not knowing what humans were," I laughed. He did not seem amused.

"I could take it off your hands," he replied. "How about one gold?"

I didn't know anything about the currency of this world, but I could tell when someone was trying to screw me over.

"No, thank you," I said and nudged the alaricorn forward with my heel.

He ran in front of me.

"Come on," he said. "What about three gold?"

"I'm fine," I continued. "You should get out of the way. You may think unicorns are nice, but alaricorns can be straight-up vicious."

I didn't actually know if either of those statements were true, but it sounded good.

"Fine then, leave. See if I care," he screamed at me. Suddenly he was upset that I wanted to leave. These humans must be fickle creatures.

The alaricorn walked up to the door and it was still closed. I didn't know how to do this without getting down, but I didn't want to face the tavern owner. I tried to nudge the alaricorn forward again. It lowered its head and a beam of magic shot out of its horn and disintegrated the door.

That was unexpected. Perhaps they were vicious. Maybe I should consider keeping it.

The alaricorn pushed onto the busy street and began to push through the crowd.

Anglachel was an enormous city. I had gone to the Fey Court with my grandmother, and it is impressive, but nothing like this! The alaricorn I was riding was surrounded by people on either side. There was some sort of outdoor market selling all sorts of various products. I thought about jumping down and trying to get something to eat, the smells filling the air were so unusual compared to the infinite autumnal cuisine I was used to, but I still had no money. I also couldn't help but notice all of the eyes glaring up at me. I think they were looking at my ears like the tavern owner.

There was a wreath of autumn flowers atop my head like a crown. I took it off and worked the weaving to make it bigger. I also fluffed up the flowers a little bit. Finally, I placed it back on my head, but now it was wide enough to cover my most prominent elven feature. I didn't want to deceive anyone, but I also wasn't trying to get killed on my first day here.

I didn't know where this crowd was taking me. Everyone appeared as though they were moving with purpose to their own individual places, yet they were all moving as a unit through this market. People were stopping at the stalls along the edges, but most of the masses were pushing in the same direction.

I didn't love this. I had run away from the Fey Realm because I didn't have any control over where my life was going. This was all a little too literal for my tastes.

I noticed an ornate-looking sidewalk heading to the right that was far less populated. I careened the alaricorn in that direction and peeled off of the crowd. I traveled past a series of buildings and was surprised to be greeted with a large green space. There was a sprawling sea of grass on either side of this sidewalk. I saw people that appeared to be around my age throwing balls back and forth, laying on blankets reading books, and doing group dances together.

I heard someone mention something about classes and I realized I was on the grounds of a school. I went to a private school in the Fey Realm that was all about how to be the perfect elven noble. It was nothing like this. These people looked free. This was the independence that I'd come here for.

As I contemplated all of this, I heard a high-pitch feminine voice directed at me.

"Is your alaricorn friendly?" a petite blonde girl asked.

If I thought the tavern owner was cute, then this girl was downright adorable. Her skin was as light and pinkish as a newborn baby. Her hair was straight and long. Her eyes shone a stunning blue. She was smiling, displaying her slightly buck teeth. She wore a fringed leather jacket over a plaid button-up shirt. The bottom of her shirt was tucked into a straight pink skirt that went all the way down to her boots. I thought she was stunning. Is this what love feels like?

"I'm sorry, I asked if your alaricorn was friendly. I'd like to pet it," the girl repeated. I hadn't responded because I'd been too busy staring at her.

"Actually, I don't know," I replied. "We only met a few hours ago."

I saw her darling face scrunch up in thought. Could she get any cuter?

"Only one way to find out," she said. I took note of her adventurous spirit, maybe I could talk her into joining me. She slowly reached her hand to the alaricorn's long mane. It leaned its head into her hand as she gave it some scratches.

Apparently, it was friendly. Good to know.

The girl looked up at me with those big blue eyes and smiled.

"I'm Traci," she said. "Pleased to meet you both."

"I'm Asha," I said. "You're the first person I've had a pleasant interaction with since I've gotten here. Nice to meet you, too."

"That's strange," she said, scrunching up her face again. "Everyone at Arcana University is usually real welcoming. What are you here for?"

"That's a complicated question," I began.

"Then why don't we go somewhere more comfortable. I can teleport us to my dorm room so you can feel free to say whatever you want," she offered.

I know that many people would say it is irresponsible to go to a second location with a stranger I'd just met, but those people have never been royals. I had gotten so used to following the person with the most authoritative voice in the room for so long, that it felt almost instinctual to go with her. That, and I didn't hate the idea of being in a room alone with the cutest girl I had ever seen in my life.

I tried to summon my most even response. "If you think that would be appropriate."

"Sure it is, everyone hangs out at each others' dorms around here," she explained.

"Then let's teleport."

She lifted her free hand up to my leg.

"May I?" she asked.

"Of course," I said, maybe a little too eagerly. It's hard to explain, but there's something about abandoning an arranged marriage that makes you want to jump into the first potential relationship you can choose yourself.

She placed her hand on my leg and I felt magical energy surround my body. Before I had time to process what was happening, we were already outside a different building.

"That was fast," I noted.

"Sure, teleportation is kinda my thing," she bragged. "Why don't we leave your alaricorn at the stables here. I can use my student ID to check it in."

I agreed and I followed along as she completed the paperwork. There was something nice about the familiarity of being told what to do. Clearly, this place was some sort of school for higher learning. Elves are always constant learners, but we usually have private tutors after we come of age. Apparently, these humans had a school for those that have just come of age. It sounded fun, but I had to remind myself that I came here for adventure, not school.

I learned through context that Arcana University was a magic school that taught magic users how to tap into the different disciplines. I'd always found my magic classes dreadfully boring, so that did help to assuage my burgeoning interest.

Traci led us up a stairway a few flights and down a hallway. We stopped at a pretty nondescript door. She pulled out a key and pushed it open.

The door may have been nondescript, but this room was not. Traci apparently had a room to herself, and it was covered in pink, and posters of various breeds of horse, unicorn, pegasus, and alaricorn. I would later discover that Traci is what humans colloquially call a "horse girl." I actually found this charming. There was something nice about categorizing people by their interests rather than their status or race.

Traci jumped on her bed and gestured to a fuzzy, foldable pink chair across from it. I took her cue and fell into it.

"So what brought you here, Asha," Traci asked.

"I'm looking for adventure," I said bluntly, like a child that was asked what they wanted to be when they grew up. That might be because Traci was the first person to actually ask me what I wanted.

"That's what a lot of people here say," she said. "Looks like you found yourself in the right place. Your clothes look lovely, but would you want to change into something a little more comfortable? I have stuff in the closet."

"I'm good for now," I said. I wanted to see just how much I could trust this girl before I dropped my guard around her.

"At least take off that flower crown. It looks really uncomfortable. It is pressing against your ears," she said with a tinge of concern.

"Do you promise you won't tell anyone?" I asked her. I remembered how we got up here, so I could run if I needed to.

"Sure," she said, puzzled.

I carefully removed the flower crown and let my long, pointed ears out.

Traci released an audible gasp. "You're an Elf."

"That I am," I responded.

"Are you going to control me? I heard that Elves do that. My parents told me," she said, clearly petrified and talking a little too fast.

"Goodness no, what is wrong with all of you people?" I answered. "I came here for adventure. Do you really think all Elves want is to enslave and control people?"

"Honestly," Traci paused. "Yes? Elves basically controlled this realm until just before I was born. This is all pretty fresh for all of us."

Suddenly, every reaction I received since arriving made much more sense. I knew that my people had their hands in a lot of different realms, but I didn't know we went around conquering them. Clearly, I was much more sheltered than I had realized. And my people did not teach us the entirety of our history. I had learned about the great artists and magical discoveries in Elven culture, but I knew nothing about our past as tyrants.

I was more than a little shell-shocked. "I didn't know that."

"Wow, you must be really confused," Traci laughed.

I appreciated her bringing levity to the situation. "You have no idea."

"Well, Arcana University was actually built to commemorate the Elves leaving this realm. The Elves taught humans magic, but always kept them at arm's length. The school opened to keep magical knowledge alive," Traci explained.

"You know a lot," I said.

"Just what every human learns in school. I'm just badly parroting what my history teacher taught me when I was little," she said modestly.

"So you're learning magic?" I asked.

"I'm trying. My spatial magic is an innate ability I was born with. I can teleport anywhere. But learning new spells has been a challenge. I hate memorizing!"

"That sounds bad," I agreed. I got through all of my school years by breezing through with my family's name. I couldn't imagine actually doing school work.

"Yeah, magic school hasn't been what I'd imagined," she confided.

"Then come with me! We can adventure together," I offered. Having someone who actually understood this world traveling with me would make all of this a whole lot easier. And if she wanted to explore our burgeoning relationship further, who am I to object?

"I can't. My parents paid my tuition. I have to finish the year out." She looked disappointed. I had her on the hook, I just had to reel her in.

"Why? You just said it sucks. And you can't tell me you wouldn't love to travel with that unicorn," I tempted. Light manipulation felt appropriate in this situation.

"Alaricorn," she quickly corrected. "But I really would!"

"Let's do it! You and me! We can take on all of—what is this world called again?" I asked, interrupting my dramatic rallying cry.

"Galevyn," Traci said.

"We can take on all of Galevyn!" I finished.

"Yeah," she said, slightly more confident now. "I can be an adventurer!"

I was sure she wouldn't blame me for this rash decision. She wouldn't agree to go with me if she didn't already want to. Logistics be damned, we were riding a high here.

"Yes, we are adventurers," I said. I couldn't believe this was really happening.

A Life of Adventure

"I just wish we didn't have to split up," Traci complained lovingly, looking at me with those big, blue eyes. It had been three months since I arrived in Galevyn, and Traci and I had become more than just friends that went on adventures together.

"I know, Trace, but I need to stay near Maxwell, and you need to keep a lookout for anything suspicious," I explained the plan to her again.

"O.K., just take care of yourself. I won't be here to save you," she teased.

"We both know that I'll be the one to do the saving," I retorted.

"Asha, we're in this together. We save each other," she repeated. This was one of our regular refrains.

"You're right. I know you're right. We save each other.". I embraced her one last time before she got into position. We gave each other a quick goodbye kiss. Traci teleported away.

Since running away from my arranged marriage and traveling to Galevyn to become an adventurer, I was surprised to find out that there was so much adventuring in the city of Anglachel. Anglachel is a massive city, and there is no shortage of businesses needing help getting rid of rodents, students needing help finding specific herbs from the Jungle of Despair, and packages that nobles wanted picked up. This wasn't exactly what I imagined a life of adventure would look like, but it was a nice change of pace from all of the ball gowns and etiquette classes.

Speaking of ball gowns, I was also surprised at how much coin I was able to get out of the one I was wearing when I came here. As long as I kept my Elvish ears hidden, the nobles in this city were absolutely fascinated with Elven culture. You'd almost think the Elves weren't mind controlling most of them just 20ish years ago. Traci and I were able to use the money from the dress to outfit ourselves in adventuring gear. She traded her "horse girl" clothes for something more practical. She now wears a human-created fabric called denim for her pants, and thank the gods; she found a way to add the cute leather fringes to those. I bought a navy blue cloak with a hood to make it easier to cover my ears. I also managed to find leather armor that had been dyed white. It really complemented the cloak and looked pretty cute. I loved it when I didn't have to sacrifice fashion for function.

The job we have found ourselves in right now has been pretty interesting. A local politician contracted us to protect him during his rallies. His name is Maxwell Canterly, and his campaign was challenging the relatively recent status quo of Anglachel. As it stood, the nobles basically ran things, and the government only really served the nobles. Canterly thought that the government should be lifting up the poorest instead of keeping them down. He said the quiet part out loud, and his competitors hated him for calling them out. Because of this boldness, he was worried that the political establishment would be coming for him. Thus far, it has been a pretty easy gig. Traci and I would stand guard, and no one really tried anything. I guess politics hasn't had time to get corrupt here yet.

I especially appreciated this job because it caught me up on Anglachelian current events. I was utterly clueless when I'd first gotten here, and Traci can only explain so much before she starts to get tired of the questions. Not to mention, this whole romantic relationship thing was a trip! Who knew having actual feelings for a person, and the physical perks that came along with it, could improve your mood so much?

I trusted that Maxwell Canterly was a progressive person who wanted to help the lower classes, and Traci seemed to agree, but truthfully, I was here for the pay. He could have been absolutely vile as long as the coin was good. I will admit, he seemed sincere enough in his speeches, and the crowds sure seemed to love him. After growing up as one of the few colorful ones in an otherwise lily-white family, it was uplifting to see so many different species of people together. His platform to expand voting rights to all citizens has rallied not just progressive human nobles but also the Halflings, Gnomes, Mascaras, and Dwarves. It was hard not to get caught up in the excitement.

I spotted Traci on top of a roof on the other side of the crowd. She would handle any threats that entered from that side. I was hidden by the stairs leading up to the stage. My job was to protect Canterly at all costs. I hadn't quite determined where my limit for "all" was yet, so I kept agreeing with him. Hopefully, it would never get that close. I began scanning the crowd, nearby alleys, and rooftops for any direct threats to Canterly. So far, so good. As he began speaking, I kept scanning, but allowed myself to tune into what he was saying.

"People of Angalchel, the revolution is not yet over!" he yelled into the crowd to uproarious applause. "The parliament thinks that their work is done. The Elves have left, and the charmed enslaved folks have been freed, but I think we all know that's not enough! Yes, Queen Florence and her lackeys were generous enough to allow the formerly enslaved to keep their shabby servants' quarters that their ancestors built in the first place. Meanwhile, she lives in her castle's lap of luxury, and the parliament's members serve from their lavish manors. I'll be the first to admit that I, too, grew up as a noble. But my eyes have been opened to the struggles of the majority of Anglachelians. It is time to accept that the government needs to be built by more than wealthy human nobles. It must be built by all of the people of Anglachel!"

The crowd once again erupted in applause. I managed to see the twinkle of metal emerging from a nearby rooftop. I leapt onto the stage and rushed to the side near the crowd. The crossbow bolt sped directly towards Canterly, and it would have hit its target if I had been just a bit slower. I pulled my aunt's sword free from its scabbard and knocked the bolt away from Canterly, in the opposite direction from the crowd. I spotted a shadowy figure shifting away from the rooftop the bolt had emerged from. I sheathed my sword and raced atop the roof. I craved adventure, and a roof chase was just what the physician ordered.

The rooftops of Anglachel are one of the few places in the city I can feel at home. The buildings here are clearly of Elven design, and standing on top of the roofs reminds me of the late nights I would look out from the window of my bedroom in the tower and imagine a life away from all the royal nonsense that became my day-to-day. It was not unusual for me to climb over my balcony and jump to the other buildings in the castle to listen in on grown-up conversations. I didn't care much about what my family members were talking about, but I enjoyed the thrill of knowing things I wasn't supposed to. This childhood pastime was one of the few skills from my old life that carried over to this new one as an adventurer. Chasing after marks on rooftops wasn't a common practice, but it did seem to happen often enough.

The cloaked figure who had shot at Canterly was about three buildings away from me. The figure was short and, while nimble, seemed to have trouble reaching the speeds my longer Elvish limbs could. The figure was throwing a grappling hook across the way so they could swing over to the next building. I knew this was my chance. I pulled a dagger from under my cloak and threw it at the rope. It didn't carve straight through the rope. Apparently, that kind of thing is really hard to do, but it did knick it on one side. It frayed the rope enough that it would at least make it a precarious leap for the figure. I raced across the rooftops between us to close the gap.

The figure looked back apprehensively as I moved closer. They appeared to be a masculine-looking halfling. He considered his options and decided to take the risk of the rope. He leaped off the rooftop, and I cringed as I saw the rope unravel a bit at the cut. It didn't snap, but it did stretch too far, altering his course. Instead of landing on the adjacent building, he dangled over its edge. I saw him quickly scurrying up the rope, but I was faster. I leaped across the gap and landed on the rooftop, my feet on either side of the rope. I drew my sword and waited for the halfling to make his way up.

I saw one set of fingertips grasp the edge of the rooftop, but the other streaked over the edge and threw a dagger in my general direction. Admittedly, I should have seen it coming. What can I say? This adventurer life is still new for me. I managed to slide away from most of it, but it did slice a neat slit across my bicep. The dagger clattered to the roof after hitting the back of my cloak. I knew it had to of punctured a hole in it.

"You asshole! This cloak is new!" I screamed at the halfling.

He sprang around the wall and landed, facing me, on the rooftop. He had another dagger drawn by the time he landed. This guy was pretty good.

"Yeah, and my plan wasn't, but you ruined it. So I guess we're even," he spat out. He gritted his teeth, ready for a fight.

I really didn't want to have to fight this guy, but at the same time, I was also excited for my first real scuffle as an adventurer. I took a defensive stance. He charged toward me, and I caught his dagger with my sword. I used his momentum to spin him onto the other side of me.

"Why are you after Canterly? You know his policies would help the Halflings of this city, right?" I asked as he readied another attack. I leap-frogged over him as he attempted to plunge his dagger into me.

"He's short-sighted," the Halfling growled. "His plans help the people of the city, but what about the people outside of it?"

I was confused. "He is running to join the parliament for the city. How would his plans have anything to do with the people outside of it?" I ducked down and swept my leg to try to trip him. He saw it coming and jumped over it. He came down hard with his dagger and almost stabbed my leg, but I managed to get it away in time.

"Typical human," he said with a level of malice I had only ever heard my grandmother use to talk about the other seasonal monarchs. "He plans to build more housing in the slums. Where is that going to go? It will have to extend into the Jungle. When Anglachel was founded, it promised the indigenous people that it would never expand into the jungle anymore."

He leapt back and chucked his dagger at my abdomen. I easily swatted it away with my sword. Either I was better than I thought, or he was losing his will to harm me.

"My dude," I began, "We live in a world of magic! Surely there must be some solution to build housing that doesn't encroach into the Jungle. I'm sure if you just talked to him. ..."

"Why would Canterly listen to me? I'm beneath him, literally and figuratively. He doesn't care what I would have to say, especially not about indigenous Anglachelians. No one seems to care about them. They always get left out of the conversation!"

The tension eased out of him a little bit. He was ready to have a conversation instead of a fight. I took advantage of it and tackled him. His body collapsed from the momentum, and I placed my foot on his chest.

Now that he wasn't a threat, the tension in my shoulders could ease a bit. "Why do you even care about the indigenous Anglachelians? Aren't they orcs, Goblins, and humans? You are a Halfling, right?"

"Yes, I'm a Halfling. It may surprise you that people can care about people that aren't themselves," he said. He meant it to be sarcastic, but it stung more than it should. I couldn't help but think about all the responsibility I ran away from in the Fey Realm. My little sister would probably have to marry that guy. Was she ready for that kind of commitment when I knew I couldn't handle it?

"Yeah, I get that," I managed to get out, a little more strained than I would have liked.

"I grew up in the slums," he explained. "I used to sneak across the border and play in The Jungle. I'm not indigenous, but I grew up with them."

"Then I'll help you. I work for Canterly; we can talk to him together," I offered. "My name is Asha. What's yours?"

"I'm The Scourge," he said in a falsely deep voice.

"You can't be serious," I laughed.

"Yes, I go by The Scourge," he repeated indignantly.

"That can't be your name. Make up a normal-sounding fake name. That's better than 'The Scourge,'" I said.

"Come on, you've got me pinned to the ground. Can you at least let me have this?" he asked. He sounded more like a young Halfling this time. I appreciated him dropping his mask around me.

"O.K.," I relented. "I'll call you 'The Scourge.'"

I searched his cloak and pockets for any additional weapons and walked back to Canterly. It felt strange to complete a mission by befriending the killer instead of offing him. Was I a bad adventurer? I decided it was best not to think about it.

Freaks Have to Stick Together

"Why didn't you go to school here?" The Scourge asked me.

Traci and I had been working with him ever since his attempted homicide at the rally. Canterly started doing less of the big public rallies, and more private events. This was probably better for his safety, but not as good for our coin pouches.

I thought back to my time in the Fey Realm and crinkled my nose. "When I came here, I had already been through enough lessons to last a lifetime."

"So you already know some magic?"

"Oh, gods no," I guffawed. "I used my magic lessons to catch up on sleep."

Traci's parents had come down from North Anglachel to visit her. She met them outside of her old dorm building because she still hadn't told them that she'd dropped out of school. I wasn't with her because she still hadn't told them about me. I'm not bitter about it.

"What got you so tired, rich girl?" he teased.

"I always stayed up late reading letters from my Aunt Poppy. I had always dreamed of coming here and being an adventurer," I confessed.

"Where's here? You're not from Anglachel?" The Scourge asked. It was an innocent enough question. He couldn't have known I was a runaway princess.

"I'm just gonna say I'm not from around here. Let me have some secrets."

"Fine, fine. I'll stop asking you about your past. For now."

We'd picked up a job to liberate a forbidden scroll of divination from Arcana University. We don't usually take jobs that might enable someone evil to destroy the world or whatever, but what harm could someone do with divination? Make money betting on a land orca race? That seemed fine. But since Traci was busy misleading her parents, The Scourge and I had to do this one on our own. Which is why we're wandering around the campus disguised as students and discussing my past. I wore one of Traci's old school uniforms with a purple blazer and a plaid skirt. The Scourge was wearing a black wizard's robe over his usual infiltration gear.

"Which one of these buildings is the library?" The Scourge inquired, looking from building to building.

"I think Traci said it was on the North Eastern side of campus near the lake. Or did she say it wasn't near the lake? Something like that," I answered.

"You don't sound too sure."

"What? I just told you I never went here. How am I supposed to know everything about the campus?"

"You could have asked Traci for directions. Or we could have done this when she's not busy. What's keeping her anyway?"

"I wish you'd stop asking so many questions," I snapped defensively. "Traci is busy. The posting had a time limit. We're the ones that are completing it. Do you need to know anything else?"

"It sounds like you've decided I don't," he said, sounding a little hurt.

I wasn't trying to hide anything from him, it was just the more he knew the more he'd have to know. Traci and I decided that it was best not to let him know I was an Elf. If he knew Traci was meeting with her parents, he would wonder why I wasn't with them. If he knew that she didn't want me to meet her parents, he would think there was something going on. He's not dumb. He'd start digging around and he wouldn't have to dig much deeper than under my hood. Or in this case, my hat. The student that I was disguised as wore a hat.

"Hey! You! Kid!" The Scourge shouted towards a passing student with long blonde hair wearing a similar uniform to mine. She stopped and looked down at him.

"Where is the library?" he demanded.

"This way, just past Meren Hall," she said automatically, pointing in a NorthEeasternly direction.

"Thanks!" I said brightly, dragging The Scourge away as the student proceeded on her way. We'd gotten lucky.

"What was that?" I said, rounding on him.

"I was figuring out where we had to go. More than you've done."

"You can be upset, but don't ruin the mission because you're mad at me. Fellow students don't usually call each other 'kid.'"

"Fine. You can do this by yourself if you want. I don't need the money that bad," The Scourge said, walking away but still in the direction of the library.

"O.K. First of all, that's a lie. We both know you need the money. Second, I want you here. I don't understand what you're so mad about."

The Scourge stopped and turned his head towards me. "I just thought we were becoming friends. I must have been mistaken."

That took me back. We'd worked quite a few jobs together in the past month, but I didn't realize he was looking for friends. I just thought we were work colleagues. Of course, it's not like I'm drowning in friends here. Running away to another realm and leaving behind everyone you've ever known will do that.

I walked up to him and knelt down so we'd be face-to-face. "Do you trust me?"

"Bloody hell, Asha. We've each saved each other's lives a couple times each now. What does it take for you to trust someone?"

"I was just giving you a chance to back out. This is going to be a lot."

A beat passed between us.

"Just tell me whatever you want to tell me!" The Scourge stated definitively.

I looked around to make sure no one was close to us, and I took off my hat. I watched as The Scourge's eyes widened, and he took a couple of big steps back.

"You're a- a- a," he stammered.

"Yes, I'm an Elf," I finished for him, securing my hat back in place.

We stayed there looking at each other for what felt like an eternity. I couldn't read his expression. He was clearly surprised, but that was all I got. Eventually, he laughed.

"Well, I guess that explains it. Traci can't introduce you to anyone in her life. You're a freak! Honestly, it's a little reassuring," he finished.

"A freak? Reassuring? I don't get you," I said, standing back up.

"That's my point! No one gets me! I'm a freak, too! We freaks have to stick together, that's the only way anything's going to get done."

"You don't have more questions? Why am I here? Who I really am?" I asked. This seemed too easy.

"Hells, Asha, I don't need your life story. I just wanted to know the reason why we were working this job alone. If the job becomes harder because the only person that knows where we're going can't be here, I want more than 'she's busy.'"

"That's actually fair." I was impressed at his practicality. "What do you say we grab a drink after this and I can fill you in on a couple of those details."

"You must have one hell of a story," The Scourge rightly presumed.

"That I do, buddy. That I do."

A Dragon in the Sewer

When I ditched my cushy arranged marriage to become an adventurer, I did not picture myself walking through the sewers of Anglachel. For the first time since coming to this world, the formal dinners and diplomatic trips seemed more appealing than what I was doing now. Walking through literal shit will do that to a person.

We ended up on this job a few months after The Scourge joined up with Traci and me. I couldn't tell what was harder to believe. The fact that one of my former enemies had become one of my closest friends or that I liked that friend enough actually to call him something as ridiculous as "The Scourge." What can I say? The little guy grows on ya'.

After the election, political bodyguard work had pretty much dried up. That meant that we had to start doing extermination jobs again. This one actually came from the first guy I'd met upon coming to Galevyn. Thank the gods he didn't remember me after I'd changed out of my ball gown. It turns out princesses are like everyone else. His name turned out to be Kyle Stringer, and his establishment had been experiencing an infestation of slugs. He said that they were mostly contained to the cellar, but every now and then, one of the sticky fellers made their way onto a table, and the patrons were not into it.

After a good hour of checking behind every barrel, crate, and shelf in the cellar, we noticed the slugs were coming out of a hole that led to a much larger chamber under the tavern. We broke through and found ourselves in the sewers of the largest city in all of Galevyn. It smelled exactly how I imagined it would. We saw a long string of slugs all headed to Stringer's place. We knew the most logical thing to do was to follow the slugs. Hence the wading through humanoid waste.

"Hey Scourge, how much longer do you think we need to go?" I asked.

"Why the hells are you asking me?" The Scourge replied.

"I don't know. You just strike me as a guy that would go creeping around in sewers."

"That feels like an insult," The Scourge said, smiling. He knew I didn't actually mean anything by it. I shrugged in his direction to complete the bit. Traci shook her head.

"This pipe should open up in a bit. We're getting pretty close to the center of the sewer system," Traci said.

"How did you know that?" I asked.

"Even I'm a little surprised at that one," The Scourge admitted.

"At Arcana University, they would have the teleport students practice in the sewers. They'd have us memorize the maps and try to teleport to specific points without having actually been there. I've not been here before, but I've definitely been forced to memorize the map," Traci said.

"I'm impressed, babe. I'd kiss you if we didn't both look and smell like shit," I complimented.

"Thank the gods for small favors," The Scourge quipped.

"I know you love us," I said to The Scourge, ruffling his hair through his hood.

"Did you just get feces all over my cloak?" he complained.

"Maybe," I said matter-of-factly. All three of us laughed. It felt good to have people to be myself around. I take back what I said about preferring to be in an arranged marriage.

We heard a loud roar ahead. We also noticed that the sewer water was getting harder to walk through.

"What was that?" Traci asked.

"Beats me. I still don't even know all the different kinds of people here, much less the monsters," I said.

"It can't be a dragon, right?" The Scourge said skeptically. "Do you think the thicker wastewater could be a clue?"

I looked down and noticed that it was actually getting thicker. It was slushy, like it was partially frozen. I also noticed a number of slugs stuck to the wall, also frozen.

I poked at one with my dagger. It was as solid as rock. "Ice is everywhere. Is that anything?"

"Blue dragons produce a cold aura," Traci said. "I learned about them in school."

Things either got even chillier, or I just shivered at the thought of fighting a dragon. Admittedly, it was scary, but I was actually pretty excited at the prospect of having a real challenge.

"Alright, guys," I began. "Let's just accept that this is a dragon. If it's not, we'll be better prepared for whatever is there."

We needed to be ready for what was ahead.

We crept forward, and the narrow pipe did open up into a large open space. Sitting in the center of the opening was a huge lizard-like creature that I could only presume was a dragon. I didn't know if we were ready for this, but I had to put on a strong front.

"We've got this, guys," I said as we prepared to fight a blue dragon.

The dragon hadn't quite noticed us yet, which gave us a quick moment to arrange ourselves strategically. We couldn't speak, as it could alert the beast, but we'd been working together long enough that we didn't need to. I spotted a great sniping location on a large pipe against the opposite wall. I pointed it out to Traci, and she silently teleported onto it. The Scourge had already slipped off, inevitably finding a hiding spot in the shadows. That only left me. I always started our fights because I was the best at getting creatures' attention. That basically meant I was the loudest. I drew my sword and took a deep breath.

"Hey ugly, come here often?" I yelled in the dragon's general direction.

Its head snapped in my direction faster than I would have thought possible and it began growling at me, but in a tone and canter that sounded suspiciously like a language. Hell if I knew what it was saying, so I charged it, raising my sword. The dragon opened its mouth, exposing its toothy maw, and a blue glow sprang in my direction. I threw my shoulder in the opposite direction and rolled away, narrowly dodging the breath attack. The wet excrement immediately froze onto my white leather armor. I grimaced, thinking about what it would take to clean it after this fight. It is true that stains on armor give it more character, but I tend to prefer blotches from the blood of my enemies as opposed to sewer water.

The dragon closed its mouth and readjusted its massive body to face me. Before it could determine its next move, Traci and The Scourge fired shots into the dragon. Or at least they tried. Traci's crossbow bolt scratched across the dragon's blue scales and splashed into the water below. The Scourge, however, managed to fire a bolt into the corner of the dragon's left eye. It raised its front claw to paw at its fresh injury, which was just the opportunity I was waiting for. I raced under it and quickly scanned for weaknesses. The majority of its scales were pretty air tight, but I did notice that at the joint connecting its claw to its torso, there was a slight gap while it had it raised. I ran towards the opposite claw and vertically scaled it, flipping in the direction of the exposed flesh. I stabbed upward before I began my descent and I could feel my blade sinking into something meaty. I held tightly to my sword to ensure my body weight would be enough to pull it free from the now-tensed dragon muscle. I landed in a crouching position and rolled backward to firmly position myself under the center of its belly.

While I was doing this, Traci had realized that sniping it wasn't going to work. She instead changed strategies and worked to guarantee The Scourge's shots did the most damage possible. She accomplished this by teleporting to an area on the top of the Dragon's back and using her spatial magic to remove individual scales from its skin. It was still a challenge for The Scourge to hit the openings, but he was doing a pretty good job.

For all of our efforts, the dragon certainly seemed annoyed with us. However, it didn't seem to be all that hurt. There was the slightest trickle of blood coming from the wound I had caused, but very little, like after someone gets a shot. We were fighting like hell against this dragon, and it felt like we were poking at it. I was starting to feel like we were a little out of our depth.

The dragon began shaking like a dog after a bath and I saw Traci fly across the room, heading towards shallow water. I sped in her direction in hopes of breaking her fall. The Scourge caught onto what I was doing and attempted to pull the dragon's attention away from me. He pulled a black powder explosive from his belt and chucked it at the dragon. He aimed his crossbow and shot a bolt at the bomb. It ignited and exploded near the Dragon's flank. Its focus shifted to The Scourge.

Meanwhile, I wasn't going to be able to reach Traci in time to catch her, but I could throw my body under her to break her fall. I dove, face up, into the water and Traci smashed into me, hard. I was sore all over, but we both were alive.

As we both crawled to our feet, we saw The Scourge was not so lucky. The Dragon had managed to spot him and now held him in its teeth. It slung The Scourge around and threw him in our general direction. I raced to break his fall the same way I had Traci's, but I could see that I was already too late. His body bounced through the muck and settled against the chamber wall. The wounds from the Dragon's fangs went straight through him. There was no surviving that. I uselessly ran to his side and cradled him in my arms.

"Scourge!" I screamed. " You're o.k., right? We can make it out."

Tears began streaming down my cheeks.

"We have to get out of here," Traci cried, kneeling at my side. I barely registered that she had said anything at all.

I felt her hand on my shoulder and the lifeless form of my friend faded before my eyes. I was in Kyle Stringer's basement, staring at the ground while my arms cradled nothing.

I bolted to my feet and rounded on Traci.

"What did you do?" I screamed. "You left him behind!"

My voice quivered and I was shaking all over.

"I can only teleport two people. You know that," she said apologetically.

"But we could have helped him," I argued. "We could have brought him out and healed him."

"He was gone, Ash," Traci said, explaining something I already knew to be true. "There was nothing more we could have done."

"But adventuring was supposed to be fun," I said blankly. "This was supposed to be fun."

Picking Up the Pieces

*I*t had been a long year since we'd fought that dragon. I used to think we were invincible. Now I know that's not true. At least not for all of us. Traci and I have been together now for a little over a year. She has been great during all of this, she was always great at taking care of people. This has brought us closer, but I don't know how I feel about it. I don't want to get close to these people if it means I could lose them at any moment. I convinced myself it was o.k. because Traci is not just "these people." She is someone that I will do whatever it takes to protect.

We continued adventuring, taking two-person jobs for a while because that was the life we lived. We didn't really have the resume to do much else. The problem was that when you'd been doing this as long as we have, people start expecting you to do more. The regular clients didn't want to keep throwing us the easy jobs because they couldn't afford to not meet the new players. Which meant they wanted to give us more dangerous jobs because they knew we could handle them. That meant we had to start finding people to add to our team again. That meant we had to spend lots of time with people I knew we would inevitably lose.

Our recruits are friendly enough. Duri is a Halfling from Yokuatsu. She risked it all to come to Anglachel on a makeshift raft with a handful of others like her. After finding homes and jobs for all of her compatriots, she had built up an impressive network of the city's criminal underground. She leveraged that to find jobs stealing very specific things for wealthy patrons. But by the time she met us, she was happy to put a bit of distance between herself and the city's crime lords.

Pegutsai is an Orc that lives in the Jungle. She knew The Scourge from way back, and we started to become fond of her after she helped us plan a tribal funeral for him. The Scourge always identified more with the natives than his family in the slums. It was what he would have wanted. When she heard that we'd been hired to harvest the pollen from a Luminescent Green Peony, she knew we'd need her help. It is a delicate process, which Duri or I could handle, but Pegutsai told us it was in a dangerous part of the Jungle. She said she could help us minimize the number of nasties we ran into.

I hated the idea of bringing someone I cared about on a job other than Traci. It's not so hard to protect one person, it gets much harder when you're trying to protect everyone. I knew I'd end up having to choose, and I was going to choose Traci. It didn't seem fair to bring Pegutsai along without her knowing that. But she was always really perceptive. There's a good chance she already had an idea of what she was walking into.

In the Fey Realm, whenever my mother would lose someone from her side of the family, she would have a painting of them commissioned. She knew she couldn't abandon her position on the Autumn Court to go home to mourn, but she did what she could from the castle. She would display the painting prominently in the family room and hang a wreath of flowers around it. She would leave it up for ten days, placing a fresh wreath of flowers each day. My grandmother hated it because it constantly reminded her that her son had married a River Elf. My mother would do it for relatives she had never met. I think it was her way of silently protesting the blatant racism of my grandmother.

I picked up a bouquet of fresh flowers from the market. Traci and I couldn't afford to have a painting commissioned of The Scourge, but luckily I have always been pretty artistic. I had sketched a number of drawings of him whenever he was alive. I removed the old flowers from around the sketch and fashioned a new wreath with the flowers from the market. Ever since The Scourge died, I'd begun a tradition of thinking about him before every job. Traci has told me that it seems excessive and that a year is too long to actively mourn, but I couldn't let myself forget the danger these jobs put my companions into. I hung the wreath around the sketch and whispered, "I'll always remember you, friend," under my breath.

Every time I go into what the people of Anglachel call "The Jungle of Despair," I can never figure out what people think is so disparaging about it. It is a lush jungle with the tallest trees and the wildest vines adorned with some of the most vibrant flowers I'd ever seen. It brings me back to my childhood when my grandmother would take me on diplomatic visits to the Spring Maiden's Duchy. My grandmother was always jealous of how much people would compliment the Spring Maiden's garden because it was so bright and colorful. As a young girl, I was often left alone outside to play. I would lose myself in the pastels while my grandmother argued over some treaty or whatever.

However, for all the beauty and magic I remembered from the Spring Maiden's garden, it couldn't hold a candle to this jungle. The Spring Maiden's garden was lovely, but it was also orderly and organized. The jungle was wild. The vines would wrap around the trees or lay along the jungle floor in no particular pattern. Some vines would be full of blooms, some would be completely barren. Some trees would grow straight up into the sky, while some trees would twist and bend in wild directions. This jungle reminded me why I came here. I didn't want to be tamed, I wanted to be free.

Before I lost myself in the trees, I directed my attention back to Pegutsai. She had been expertly darting around the brambles, and the rest of us just had to follow. I'd always heard stories about adventurers traveling through thick jungles like this by cutting a path, but Pegutsai knew the jungle well enough that we didn't have to damage the wildlife. I loved it. It felt like we were sneaking through secret passages. I stayed in the back of the group so that I could make sure to keep an eye on Traci. She struggled a bit more than the rest of us, she didn't need to be flexible when she teleports everywhere. But she was keeping up today. I was proud of her.

Traci's hand grasped a branch to her right, and I saw two small glints creeping down toward her hand. I slid down the muddy incline and swatted up with the broadside of my sword. The snake went flying through the air, and the branch snapped. I scooped Traci up and continued sliding down the incline, stopping at an adjacent tree.

"What the hell, Ash?" Traci rounded on me.

"There was a snake about to bite you! I was saving you!" I said, defending myself.

"You think I didn't see it? It was halfway up the branch. I wasn't planning on staying there long enough for it to get to me."

"I just didn't want to take any chances."

Traci gave me the same look of pity and acceptance I'd gotten many times this past year. "I know, Ash, but you've got to let me make my own decisions."

I knew what she meant. I had been jumpy lately and swooping in without thinking. She needed to be able to act for herself when we're on jobs. I took a step back and a deep breath.

"You're right. I'm sorry," I relented.

The rest of the journey was pretty uneventful until we came to a wide river. As Traci and I approached, Pegutsai had begun testing the strength of the long vines.

"We're going to have to swing across," she explained. "Are you going to be o.k.?" she asked, looking at Traci.

"Yeah, it's fine," Traci said. "I can just teleport across. No big deal."

I didn't like the sound of that. "Shouldn't you save your teleports in case we actually have to fight?"

"I mean, just one shouldn't take too much of my magic," Traci assured me.

"Let's be safe. You know that I could swing both of us across. We just have to tie you to me," I suggested.

"You're sure that will work?" Traci questioned. "You'll be fine?"

"C'mon babe, you know me. I've got this," I boasted.

We used some rope to tie us together. Duri used some knots I'd never seen before to make sure Traci was secure. I let Pegutsai and Duri go first. They had to switch vines about three times to make it across. I watched the rapids of the river rage below. I couldn't let us fall. Traci was tied in so tight, she'd have no way to swim out of it. I bounced on the balls of my feet a couple of times to try to get used to the new weight. Traci wasn't heavy, but she was a bit bigger than me. That means she more than doubled the weight I was used to when I'd do this sort of thing. I was starting to get a little nervous, but I still knew it was smarter for Traci to conserve her magic.

"You o.k.?" Traci asked. She could probably feel my heart racing since she was snug against my back.

"Yeah, just getting excited," I lied.

Pegutsai and Duri had safely made it across and it was our turn. I took several steps back so I could get a running jump. I raced towards the river bank and used the momentum to propel us forward as I grabbed the first vine. We shot forward like an arrow freshly loosed from a bow. Our arch was much faster than I'd anticipated. We reached the peak of the swing in a matter of seconds. I quickly readjusted and took hold of the next vine. It wasn't ready for the sudden shift and took a wide swerve to the right. I suddenly didn't know where we were going, because the vine was heading to an open space, away from the other hanging vines. I released a panicked inhale that Traci must have heard.

"Don't worry, I've got this," she said. Suddenly, the added weight disappeared from my back. Traci must have teleported to the other side of the bank. I used the opportunity to take a wild leap towards a bundle of vines straight ahead. I'd made it and I was able to scurry my way across to my waiting companions.

I rushed up to Traci and took her into my arms.

"I'm so sorry, I don't know what I was thinking," I cried.

"It's o.k. Ash. I'm sorry too, I know you wanted me to save my magic," she apologized.

"No, it's my fault. I'm so scared all the time. I don't want to lose you," I finally said out loud.

"Ash, I'm not going anywhere," she said, confused.

"No, not like that. I just want to make sure you're safe."

"I know what you mean. I miss The Scourge too." That eased the constant pit that had been in my stomach. "But this is our life. We chose to be adventurers. I know what I signed up for, and you have to let me live my life."

"I'm just so scared," I repeated.

"Me too. I don't want to die, or lose you, or Duri, or Pegutsai. But if this is going to work, we have to trust each other. And trust each other to make our own decisions," she pleaded.

"I just miss him so much," I said. I began to cry and rested my head on her shoulder.

"I know, Ash, I know," she said.

Would That Really Be So Bad?

Traci

"It's for a set of twins, magic users in The Slums," Ulani said, finishing the job offer. Ulani was a Mascara, with yellow skin and antlers like a deer. She'd been giving us job tips for the past couple of years.

"It's a lot of gold, Trace," Asha commented.

"But we don't really need the gold, Ash," I reminded her. As I started getting older, and Asha really didn't, we started to settle down a little bit. We'd made a good bit of coin adventuring, and we bought a house on the northeast side of Middle Anglachel. Many of our companions were able to retire, and about as many weren't so lucky. Now that it was just the two of us again, we were able to be pretty selective on the jobs we took. "Is this really the kind of job we want? What did they even do?"

"The official job offer doesn't say, it just has their names and descriptions," Ulani answered.

"I think you know I'm not asking about the official job offer. You've had to have heard people talk about them," I said, trying to coax the truth out of her.

"Only because it's you, Miss Traci." Ulani sighed. "You know you've always reminded me of my mother."

I could have done without that last bit. I really didn't think about the long-term consequences of being in love with an Elf. It was getting pretty annoying when people started mistaking me for Asha's aunt or mother. We were the same age, but she only looked about three years older than when I'd first met her. To most people, at least. I could always see the years of pain and hardship in her.

"People say that they're messing with the balance of power in the city," Ulani began. "See, the girl, Quinn, she can do necromancy magic. She's been using it to heal up people in The Slums. It's taking business away from the doctors in the market. The boy, Quincy, he can do holy magic. He's been putting blessings on people, and they've been staying healthier. The factory owners in the Business District hate it."

"Why?" Asha asked. "I thought all they cared about was productivity.

Wouldn't they be happy that their workers can come in more often?"

"If you're going to pick 'em this young, Miss Traci, you should at least make sure they're smart," Ulani said with a laugh. Asha looked back at me and smiled. She thought it was funny when someone called her young.

"Why don't you go ahead and answer her question, Ulani?" I said.

"Sure, sure. The factories count on their staff getting sick or breaking down by the time they reach middle age. If they quit before they get old, they can trade them in for someone younger. If their staff stays healthy, they're going to get old. Even if they stay as productive, they have to pay them more for their years of experience," Ulani explained.

"So the millionaires in the city want to nip this in the bud before they lose too much money," I reasoned.

"That's evil," Asha said.

"Maybe she is smart," Ulani said.

"You said they are magic users, but they live in The Slums. Did they go to Arcana University on a scholarship?" I asked.

"No, no, Miss Traci. These two aren't even old enough to have started at the university. They must have been born with their magic."

That struck a chord. "So they're like me."

"What do you think, Trace?" Asha asked.

"Let's take the job," I told Ulani.

"Really? You gonna take them down?" Ulani said, surprised.

"Something like that," I said.

Ulani gave us all the information she had about the job. My magic had gotten a lot stronger after the 30 years we'd been adventuring, and Asha finally stopped worrying so much about me using up my power. I teleported us to a fancy office in the Business District, and we negotiated a higher pay rate with the client. Apparently, they really do pay more for experience. I made sure the contract was worded so that we would "take care" of them. I've learned that vague wording is a lifesaver in these kinds of jobs. I teleported us to the edge of The Slums, and we began walking to the location of the twins' most recent pop-up clinic.

"We're saving them, right?" Asha said, knowing the answer already.

"Of course," I said. "These two are obviously doing what they think is the right thing. They shouldn't be killed for that. You know the other adventurers in town wouldn't think twice about it."

"Oh, I know," Asha said. "And they'll be great assets. Necromancy and holy magic are pretty rare. Especially when it's innate. Think of how easy it would be to clear out undead with them!"

"This isn't a recruitment trip. We want to help them choose what they want for themselves," I chided Asha. She'd been like this for a few years now. I knew she loved me, but it felt like everybody else was a resource for her. She'd stopped caring about anyone that wasn't us.

"Sure, but you know they'll want to be adventurers," Asha countered. "What kind of a life is there for two young people with powerful magic that's not this life?"

"I don't know," I said. "Maybe we could pay for them to get into the university?"

"Are we adopting these kids?!" Asha guffawed.

"Would that really be so bad?" I asked. "To have a couple of people to look after us when we grow old?"

"I think you mean when you grow old," Asha said.

"You're just as old as I am," I reminded her. "You're going to start slowing down, too."

"Whatever you say, babe," Asha said before jogging ahead to check the cross street in front of us.

This was far from our first time in The Slums, but it was always a little unsettling. Since my family lived in North Anglachel, I had always heard about the rampant crime in The Slums. As I'd gotten older, I realized that it was mostly because the majority of non-humans, as well as darker-skinned humans, lived in The Slums. It is wild to realize how deeply engrained a lot of this stuff is. I'm sure the fact that The Slums is also the home of rampant poverty is also a factor. The streets are not as well-kept, the houses are not as well-maintained, and the people are, I'll say, less refined. I had learned to find the beauty in The Slums over the years. Most of it resided with its people.

It took us a while to ask around and figure out where the twins would be, but we eventually got word that they would be setting up a pop-up clinic that night in an abandoned warehouse at The Docks.

"Why's it always a warehouse in The Docks?" Asha asked, laughing.

"You've gotta love the classics," I said. "At least they're not doing evil things there."

We had taken out more than our fair share of criminal activity in The Docks. The Docks are adjacent to The Slums, but it is mostly the center of shipping operations in Anglachel. That also leads to an increased level of business activity as compared to The Slums. The shadiest folks in Anglachel have learned that if you want to stay out of sight, passing through The Slums is the most effective way to do that. I resented how right they were.

"What they're doing is still illegal, Trace," Asha reminded me. "They don't have a permit to run a magic business here. What the rich guys are doing is wrong, but that doesn't make what they're doing right."

"Since when did you care so much about the law? Aren't you the same Asha Alistar that stole 5,000 gold from the Bank of Anglachel because a teller was rude to you once?" I asked.

"It was for more than that, but yeah, pretty much," she admitted. "O.K., so they're helping people illegally, who cares? They probably don't know any better."

I grinned and nodded in approval. "Now you're getting it."

"Let's go adopt these kids!" Asha said, racing ahead and throwing her fist into the air.

Hearing her say it made me feel warm inside. She actually wanted to let new people into our life. Really let them in. Maybe she wasn't changing so much after all.

We finally found the warehouse. It was, as expected, the most blighted one we could find. I'm pretty sure we've been to this exact warehouse at least three times in the past decade. We decided I should go in first. I could teleport in and try to explain what we were doing here. Asha would sneak in the back and provide backup if they weren't initially receptive to our offer.

I looked through the front window, and I spotted a locked door outlined in light. They were here. I teleported to the door and knocked.

A high-pitched feminine voice called out from behind the door. "Look, I don't know how you got in here, but we're not open yet."

"Quinn, I'm here to speak with you. I think you'll want to hear what I have to say," I called through the door.

"Lady, I don't know who you are, but we are busy," a similarly high-pitched masculine voice yelled.

"I'm giving you a chance to come out here on your own, I don't want to drag you out of here." I tried. I didn't want to threaten them, but they were clearly already on guard.

"Try us, lady!" Quincy snapped.

I teleported the door off its hinges, to reveal the twins setting up chairs in a large room. They were just setting up for their clinic. They were humans with light skin and dark hair. Quincy's hair was combed to the left side and draped in front of his eyes. Quinn's hair was long, with bangs perfectly framing her face. They were really thin. Free clinics must pay as much as it sounds.

"I warned you!" Quincy shouted at me. He lifted his hand towards me, and it began to glow with a bright light.

"I wouldn't if I were you," Asha's voice growled. She was suddenly standing behind Quincy with a sword held to his throat.

"Please, we don't want any trouble," Quinn said, panicked. "We just want to help people."

"I know that," I said, trying to reassure her. "We don't want any trouble either."

"Your friend's sword tells a different story," Quincy said. His eyes were moving wildly, trying to catch a glimpse of his assailant without actually moving his head.

"Drop your hand, and I'll move the blade away from under your chin," Asha said authoritatively.

Quinn and Quincy looked each other in the eyes for what felt like an eternity. Finally, Quincy lowered his hand.

"Was that so hard?" Asha asked, slowly returning the blade to its scabbard.

"They're scared, give them a little slack," I begged her.

Asha held her hands up, relenting to me. "Fine."

"Who are you? What are you doing here?" Quinn asked carefully. It felt like she was not sure what she was supposed to do.

"We were hired by some really powerful people in this city. They don't like what you're doing in The Slums," I explained, trying to keep any inflection out of my voice. I wanted to give them the information without giving away what we thought about it.

"So why not just kill us?" Quincy asked. "Clearly, the two of you could have just done that without much trouble."

Asha audibly laughed from the back of the room. "You got that right."

"I'm like you," I explained. "I was born with the power to use spatial magic. I know what it's like not to understand your own power."

"We don't need your help," Quincy said, a little too quickly.

"Quince, I would like to learn how to control my power," Quinn said, pleading with her brother. "I almost made Mrs. Meadows a zombie. What would we have done if that happened?"

"We'd have figured it out. I could have blasted it with my holy magic," Quincy said.

"And kill everyone at the clinic? You've never been able to control your blasts either," Quinn retorted.

I began slowly walking up to Quinn.

"I can help you," I said. "It has taken me years to learn how to control my magic. I can teach you how I did it."

"Why would you help us? Do these 'powerful people' want to use us?" Quincy asked.

"I'm sure they'd love to," Asha quipped. "But we don't. We want to make them think you've been taken out. We'll still get paid, but we can help the two of you build a new life."

"Why should we trust you?" Quincy asked, narrowing his eyes at Asha.

"Maybe because I didn't kill you when I had the chance?" Asha offered. "If you don't trust us, you're going to die. Not at our hands, but they're just going to hire someone else. After decades of doing this, I can confidently say we're the most merciful mercenaries in the business."

"Decades? How old are you? You look like you're our age?" Quinn questioned.

"We'll explain everything," I said. "But we have to get out of here. If we could find you, it is only a matter of time until someone else does too."

"Could we do the clinic?" Quincy asked, suddenly more sincere. "There are people counting on us. This can be our last one, but there are promises we made last time that I want to keep."

"Asha, what do you say? Can we play bodyguard for one night?" I asked.

"Honestly," Asha began, "Sounds like fun."

"O.K., so we have a deal?" I asked. "We keep you and your patients safe for one night, and you'll come with us."

"Deal," Quinn said, clearly before her brother could chime in.

I felt really good. We'd done it. We saved these two kids, and Asha seemed willing to get to know them better. I started to feel like my worry might have been misguided. I might have been seeing things in Asha that I expected to see, instead of what was actually there. She pulled Quincy aside and it made me smile. She must have seen some of herself in him. I certainly did.

"So you're interested in learning more about zombies?" I overheard her ask him.

For the Rest of Your Life

I t's not always easy being an Elf in a human world. They never use enough seasoning on their food. It feels like all of their cultural traditions revolve around money. They keep saying things like "life is short," when it just isn't for me. They just grow old too fast. When someone says they'll love you for the rest of their life, you'd like to think that they'll be around for the rest of yours. For an Elf in a human world, that is just not how things work.

Traci and I have lived what many in Galevyn would consider a full life. We've made so many friends and lost about half as many. We made a lot of money and bought a house. We raised two teenage magic users into successful adult adventurers. We even saved the world a couple of times. We were two very accomplished individuals, but Traci was nearing the end of her life, and I still have several centuries left in me. I loved this place because it moved so fast; now I understood why.

Traci's lying in our bed right now, and the doctors say she could go at any minute. It's so bizarre. She doesn't even seem that sick. She's just old. It is so confusing that this woman, one of the most powerful women on the planet, can leave it the same way as everyone else. Didn't we do enough to earn her more time? Was there something else we could have done?

The door to our bedroom opens, and Quincy walks out. He's become a lot closer to us ever since his sister died. His face looks like he's come to terms with what is happening. He is still sad, but there is some sense of acceptance there.

"You should go see her," he tells me.

"I know," I respond.

"She's getting worse. You should be by her side," he says, telling me things I already know.

I slowly stand up and make my way to the door. He puts his hand on my shoulder and pulls me in for a hug.

"I know this is hard, Mom. We'll get through this together," he reassures me.

I return the hug and consider what he said. He expects me to stick around. He wants me to watch him grow old and leave me too. I rest my head on his shoulder and consider this. How much do I owe him? I lift my head and nod, trying to conceal my indecisiveness. I walk into the room, and I see her.

It is so strange how, thinking back, she looks nothing like the girl I met on the campus of Arcana University. Even so, every time I look at her, all I see is my Traci. The woman that stood by me even when I made the wrong choices. The woman who made me better by calling me out when I needed it. The woman I love more than any other person I've ever met. My Traci.

"Hi, Ash," she rasps when she sees me approach.

"You look great, babe," I say. I mean it. As I said, I see her for who she is, and she'll always be beautiful to me.

"Yeah, but I don't hold a candle to you. What did I do to deserve to grow old with someone as incredible as you?"

This is too much. I can feel tears forming in my eyes.

"I could ask you the same thing," I say, sitting in the chair next to her bed and grasping her hand.

"Can you sit with me?" she asks.

"For the rest of your life," I agree, knowing it won't be much longer.

"I love you, Ash," she says with one of her final breaths.

"I love you too, Trace," I reply. I lean in and kiss her. Really kiss her. Her head lifts to meet mine, even though she doesn't really have the strength. I want to hold onto this moment for as long as I can.

I don't know how long we held hands. It could have been minutes, it could have been hours, hell, it could have been days. All I know is that I eventually fell asleep, and when I woke up, she was gone. Her body was still there, obviously, but Traci was gone.

I walked to our closet and grabbed a pre-packed bag I keep in there. It held several days worth of clothing, my adventuring supplies, and enough gold to last me for a few months. I walk to the corner of our room and fasten my sword harness to my belt. I flashback to the moment I strapped the sword around my ridiculous ball gown before leaving the Fey Realm. I guess this is the start of a new chapter for me.

I walk out of our room, and I see Quincy sitting there. I dig the house keys out of my pocket.

"The house is yours, Quince," I tell him, handing him the keys.

"You can't leave, Mom. You have to process this. We need to make arrangements for her funeral together," he says.

"You know that I don't work like that. I appreciate you so much. You and your sister reminded me that connections are worth making, but I can't stay here. I can't see her in every wood grain on the floor, every room, every person," I say, touching his cheek. "I can't lose you, Quincy. I want to live believing you're still out there, somewhere. I want to be able to pretend that in 50 years, there's still someone I love living a fulfilling life."

"I can't understand. I don't think I could ever understand, but I believe you," he says. "Find happiness, Mom. Don't give up on people. Make friends, fall in love again."

"I will," I say, knowing that I'll never let myself fall in love again.

I hug him one last time and walk out the door. I risk one final look back. I see myself carrying Traci across the threshold. I see Quinn and Quincy seeing the house for the first time and confiding in us that this will be the first time either of them will have their own bedroom. I see all 25 adventuring companions that walked through our door at some point in the last 40-some years. Then I turn around and face the road before me. I won't forget these memories, but I can't dwell on them. There's a lot of life ahead of me.

Keep Moving Forward

"You are so beautiful," Rio whispered into my ear as he moved his smooth hand from the back of my head to the small of my back. I took a deep breath and drank him in. He smelled like sweat and myrrh from the oils he used in his rituals. The scents clung to his thick chest hair. I saw his muscles tense under his tan skin, and he released a held breath just before he rolled over onto the bedroll spread out in our tent.

"You're incredible," he told me for the fifth time that day.

I sat up and began putting my clothes back on, then I looked back at him and flashed a grin. "You may have mentioned that before."

He looked up at me with sad puppy-dog eyes. "C'mon, Asha. You don't have to leave. You could lay here with me for a little while. We only just set up camp. We have time."

He's not the first partner to say something like this to me. I hoped I could talk him out of it. I'd hate to have to shut this down before we'd completed the job. That'd be awkward as hell.

"We agreed this was just about fun, didn't we?"

"Of course, but I just hoped. . .uh . . . I mean . . . ." he began to stumble. He's especially cute when he's frazzled. His rolling Reyes accent is still attractive when it doesn't know what to say. This wasn't helping.

"We can talk later," I said evanescently, hoping he'll forget this conversation happened.

I finished the last buckle on my black leather armor and walked out of the tent. My long dark hair was down and still a bit of a mess. Lisel and Ricci were sitting around the fire. Lisel is a Halfling alchemist, meaning she makes things that heal us and things that hurt our enemies. I've worked with a lot of different magic users in my century and a half of adventuring, and she's the first that doesn't actually perform it. She stores it in bottles. I still don't really understand magic. She's a traditional mother friend, always trying to look out for us. Her look complements her personality, with smudges covering her clothes and her chestnut hair sticking out in all directions. Ricci is a red Mascara with rounded goat-like horns outlining his surprisingly soft facial features. He has raven black hair and a rough beard. He does most of the upfront fighting for our group.

I sidle up to the fire and take a seat on a rock. "So what are we thinking? Will we make it to Ahranai tomorrow morning?"

We're in Kapoor tracking down a High Priest of a Quietus cult. He has been terrorizing a small town called Ahranai, and the town secretly commissioned a job posting through the thieves' guild to stop him. Lisel, Ricci, and Rio were surprised that I wanted to do something that seemed so altruistic for such low pay, but the truth is that I take every opportunity I can to leave Anglachel. Too many memories there.

"I'm thinking you should start taking it easier on our paladin," Ricci's deep growl of a voice teased. "Some of his screams started to worry me."

I laughed with him. "You probably won't need to worry about that much longer."

"Take it easy on her," Lisel said, slapping Ricci's arm with the back of her hand. "Yes, Asha, we should make it to Ahranai by tomorrow morning. Have either of you thought about our strategy?"

Ricci straightened his posture, suddenly serious. "I spent a lot of time in Ahranai in my youth. I know the city layout pretty well. That should be to our advantage."

"Yes, good. Asha, what have you prepared?"

"Wait, no, we're not just going to move on. Ricci, you grew up in Ahranai? How are we just now hearing about this?" I asked.

I looked into his eyes, and his seriousness was still holding, but only just. "I didn't grow up in Ahranai. But I used to visit family there. It's not a big deal. We don't need to talk about it."

"Of course," Lisel said, trying to keep the meeting on track. "Now, Asha, what do you think will be the best strategy to draw out the high priest?"

"Oh, we're going to talk about it," I said, continuing the conversation I wanted to have. When you don't actually get that close to anybody, it is pretty fun to dig into their pasts. "I didn't even know there were still Mascara in Kapoor. I thought they got rooted out during the River Elves' partition."

"Well, my bubbe was always stubborn. Her family had lived in that house for generations, and she wasn't going to get shoved out for being different."

"I get that, but how could she have stopped them? I've heard stories from other Mascara about some pretty brutal treatment when they resisted the River Elves."

That question surprisingly brought a smile to his face. "She was born with the ability to use barrier magic, and she'd mastered it enough to hold a barrier around the house." This was obviously a point of family pride for him.

I whistled, acknowledging how impossible what he was describing must have been. "She sounds like a spitfire." She reminded me of Traci. I blinked hard to shut the memory out of my head.

"She is," Ricci said, settling back into his serious posture to continue the strategy meeting.

"But yeah, I'm prepared to fight. I plan to sneak around and slit the throat of the high priest when he comes out. You know what I do," I finally contributed.

"Thank you for all your preparation," Lisel said sarcastically. "Did anyone put any thought into how we'd draw him out?"

Rio slinked out of the tent and sat next to me, a little closer than I would have preferred. "I could pretend to be a paladin of Quietus. That should certainly pique his interest."

"Thank you, Rio," Lisel commended. "That is an actual idea."

******

The following morning we packed up and made our way down the dirt road to Ahranai. Lisel was right. It wasn't long until we saw buildings in the distance. Unexpectedly, we also saw smoke rising from the inland side of the town. Before any of us could ask any questions, Ricci took off in that direction. I chased after him because I knew I was the only one that could keep up with the most athletic member of our party. I looked back to see Lisel give me a nod, acknowledging she understood that I'd look out for him if anything came up. We ran until we pushed into a smoke cloud. I slowed down to assess what we were running into, but Ricci didn't stop. He reached the charred remains of a house that had crumbled into itself. He threw himself into the ashes and began digging frantically through the rubble. I carefully approached him and knelt down.

"Ricci, what's going on?" I said in the most neutral tone I could manage.

"Bubbe. . . . This is where . . . What if she—? " he stammered. Gods. This neighborhood was where his grandmother lived. This was a massive attack and there is pretty much no way she made it out.

I put my hand on his shoulder. "Ricci, buddy, we need to get out of this smoke before we lose our breath. You've got to be feeling it."

He continued to mindlessly dig, but I could see him breathing much heavier. I put my hands on either side of his face and forced him to look at me.

"We'll figure out what happened, but we can't do that if we're dead. Let's get out of here and ask around."

He slowly nodded and I helped him stand up. I still couldn't see any trace of his firm foundation that our group had learned to rely on. He was fragile. Broken. I was familiar with that feeling. I wrapped my arm around his torso and walked him out of the blackened hull of his bubbe's neighborhood.

When we emerged into the fresh air, Rio and Lisel were there to meet us.

Rio rushed up. Gods, I could not deal with his doting now. "Is he o.k.? Ricci, are you o.k.? You look burnt."

Oh, he was checking on Ricci. That was refreshing.

"He's fine, he just panicked." I didn't know how much Ricci wanted me to say yet.

"Yes. I'm fine," Ricci said. His countenance shifted from worry to determination. "We need to find who did this."

"I'll ask around," I offered. Lisel and Rio were better at the emotional stuff anyway. Getting answers was something I could do. I slipped away before anyone could object. I risked a look back and I saw them entering an inn at the edge of town.

I began asking around town and it didn't take too many questions to learn that the spirited older Mascara woman living in that neighborhood didn't make it out. It seemed she'd become a fixture of the town. She was the only one who was willing to stand up to the cult's high priest, and clearly, this destruction was how he felt about it. They said the entire neighborhood went up in flames at the same time. She lived in the middle, with everything around her on fire, she never stood a chance. This was very targeted. The city had already dug through her house and they couldn't find any substantial remains, just ashes. Regular fire can't do that, this had to be magic. I was tempted to go after the high priest on my own, but Ricci needed to see this through. He deserved that much.

I returned to the inn to see the three of them sitting around the common room. Kapoor has always been known for its colorful and elaborate patterns. This room was no different. It featured two couches with an orange repeating circular pattern. As I got closer, I could see it was an artistic representation of leaves. Life is full of ironies. The couches were facing a crackling fireplace. It looked like the inn had closed off this room to give us some space. Based on their faces, Ricci had filled the other two in on what he presumed happened.

Lisel looked up at me as I approached. "What did you find out?"

"This was them, the Quietus cult. It was definitely a magical fire and apparently, Ricci's bubbe was pushing back against their demands."

"That sounds like her. Did she . . ?" The question faded before he could say the words. I just shook my head. He didn't need to hear me say it. It would just make it hurt more. His eyes were still focused, but I saw moisture gather at the base of them. I walked up and sat beside him. I just wanted to be here for him, whatever he needed.

"We can take the night off," Lisel concluded. "If they just acted, that should buy us some time before their next move. Let's get some rest."

"No!" Ricci shouted. "We have to do something now."

"Yes," Lisel agreed. "We do have to do something now. I have to prepare some alchemist fire and potions for the upcoming assault. Rio needs to finish the Quietus alterations to his armor. Asha needs to continue asking around to learn what she can about the cultists. You need to take a beat. You are of no use to us if you can't think clearly. Let yourself grieve, at least a little bit, then you can help us when the time comes."

Rio stood up, taking Lisel's cue to walk out of the room to work on his disguise. Lisel looked at me like she was trying to figure out what I was feeling. I didn't want to think too much about the emotions this was brewing inside of me, but her eyes were pulling it out of me.

"It's never easy," I finally said. Ricci turned towards me, tears visibly rolling down his face. "To lose someone. I've lost my fair share of people in my life. Some of them meant a lot to me, probably as much as your bubbe meant to you. And one of them certainly meant more."

Now I could feel tears welling up on my face. For the first time in decades, I didn't push it down.

"It doesn't matter how they go, it never seems fair. It always feels like a personal attack, like the gods are playing some sort of cruel joke on you. I mean, they put people into my life for what? To take them away? How does that make sense? But we have to keep moving forward. That's all we can do."

Massive tears were now pouring down my face and I could hear the breaks they caused in my voice. I couldn't believe I was being this vulnerable.

"She's right, Ricci. We have to keep moving forward, for those we've lost. We have to live the best life we can, because they can't. Because that is what they'd want," Lisel said, clearly speaking to both of us. For some reason, her words made me angry.

"How do you know what she'd want!" I shouted, louder than I meant to be.. "I held her hand as she died. I watched the life leave her body. The last thing she told me was that she loved me. She didn't say anything about what kind of life I was supposed to lead."

"Did you know my grandma?" Ricci said, clearly still disoriented. Lisel looked confused too, but she was trying to follow what I was saying.

"How long ago was this?" she asked me gently.

"64 years, three months, and twelve days," I said, almost automatically, tucking my hair behind my Elven ears.

Lisel stood up and threw her arms around me. "Oh, Ash. You've held this in for that long?"

I couldn't say anything. Her Halfling height meant I could still see over her head. I looked in Ricci's direction and his eyes had gone wide, clearly trying to understand all the revelations I'd just thrown at him. The expression in his face was ridiculous, especially with the tear tracks still visible on his cheeks. He looked like a crying child suddenly surprised by a new dog. It made me laugh.

"What is it?" his low voice rumbled.

"Your face," I managed through my hysterical bouts of hysteria.

His hand began to feel around his face. Lisel looked at him and started to laugh too.

"What?" he asked.

"She's right, your expression. It's not like you," Lisel explained.

Ricci didn't seem to understand, but at this point the laughter was contagious. He joined us and we sat there laughing with each other. I felt like I was releasing 64 years of built-up tension. After a few minutes, we regained our composure.

Lisel slapped my arm with the back of her hand. "You've got to tell people your secrets. If this is going to work, we have to trust each other."

I smiled at hearing Traci's words repeated to me. I resisted the urge to push her out of my mind and I allowed her memory to comfort me.

"I trust you," I said to Lisel and Ricci, and I meant it. I'd been moving through life like a ghost. Jumping from group to group and never forming any real attachments. I remembered the day I'd lost Traci, and Quincy urging me to make friends and fall in love again. I owed it to Traci to try. I still didn't know if I could fall in love, but I could start letting people in again.

"You guys want to hear how an Elven Princess of Autumn traveled to Galevyn to become an adventurer?"

"That sounds like a story my bubbe would have loved," Ricci said.

I didn't want to lose these people, but I finally remembered what it felt like to have someone to lose.

"My Aunt Poppy was an adventurer, and she'd always tell me stories about this realm. One day, I was dueling with her . . . . "

Karuk

A Third Option

Growing up as an Orc of the Hukawan tribe, it was drilled into me how much the people of Anglachel feared us. The humans of our tribe could get away with a bit more, but because Orcs were big and scary and different, we had to be very careful within the city. We couldn't avoid it all together, hunting parties had to enter the city to trade furs and leathers for the things our tribe needed that the jungle couldn't provide. The people of Anglachel accepted that small groups of Orcs would briefly enter the city, but they would always travel as a group, do their business, and leave. My father reminded me of this before I joined him for my first trip into the city. This was an important milestone every hunter crosses on their sixteenth birthday.

The Hukawan hunters wear thin leather armor because it takes a lot of flexibility to easily move around the jungle. They all carry bows, arrows, and hand axes. Most hunters tend to favor one weapon or the other. My father, Tanwe, tended to prefer his ax and he has been training me to use it since I was very young. I always liked the way my green skin paired with the light brown armor.

My father had been to the city of Anglachel many times. He had told me about the large buildings, and the delicious aromas drifting out of the windows of restaurants, and the hustle that touched every part of the city. I knew to expect that the city was a much different place from the jungle. I didn't expect to see so many different kinds of people.

I saw the fear I had learned about early on. If I followed the eyes of humans passing us on the street, I noticed that they stopped on the tusks of the adult hunters. I spotted a Halfling mother walking with her two children a couple of blocks ahead of us. Her face tensed when she spotted us and then she hurried her children across the street so they wouldn't have to pass us. Those sorts of moments were frequent enough that it was impossible to miss.

However, what piqued my interest were the children playing together in the open lots where shacks used to be. A Halfling girl, much like the one forced to flee from us earlier, kicked a red ball. It rolled across the dirt and a large boy, a Giant, raced towards it. He scooped up the ball and chased after the girl. She was giggling as she ran between his legs and he bent down to attempt to tag her with the ball. As she emerged on the other side of him, he lost his balance and tumbled to the ground.

"No fair!" His voice boomed throughout the city streets. "You're too little. It is too hard to reach you."

"Shut up, Pyson. You've caught me before. You just have to do better!" The Halfling girl said encouragingly.

Pyson, the Giant boy, reached his massive arm around and grasped the leg of the Halfling girl. She also stumbled and fell to the ground beside him.

"Got you, Tini!" he declared.

"That is cheating, Pyson," she said, laughing and rolling towards Pyson.

"Maybe a little," he said as he turned his head in Tini's direction, also laughing.

I couldn't understand why these children who were so different could play together without fear, when everyone was so terrified of people like me. Tini began to stand up and dust herself off when she noticed me staring at them.

"Hi! Do you want to play with us?" she said, sounding so innocent. She didn't realize that she was supposed to be scared of me. It felt nice. I knew I couldn't stay. I turned to continue walking with the hunting party, butthey were gone. I was so distracted watching them play that I'd lost the hunting party.

"I'm sorry, I have to go," I shouted across the street to Tini and ran down the sidewalk.

"It's o.k. We can play later!" Pyson said, sitting up.

It made me a little sad to know that I never could. I waved in their general direction as I sprinted down the block to find my father's hunting party. I stopped at the corner and looked in every direction and I couldn't see them anywhere. I looked down the sidewalk on all four sides and they looked the same. A dirty, concrete sidewalk littered with garbage while grass grew in between the individual slabs of rock. I turned left, because I wouldn't have to cross the street and I knew I had to keep moving. I could probably get out of the city on my own, but I was terrified of what would happen if someone with authority recognized me as an Orc in the city by herself.

As I began walking down the block, I started to hear muffled sniffling. I looked down an alley as I passed and I could hear the sound more clearly. I stalked down the alley, following the cries. I approached a discarded chair and moved it to the side. My locked eyes with a terrified Goblin child that looked to be about the same age as me.

The Goblin had yellow-green skin and wore gray wolf furs crafted into a shirt and pants, featuring buttons made of chestnut shells. He was in a seated fetal position, hugging his knees against his chest. His hair was a very pale yellow, but with vibrant blue and red streaks running through it, tied into a high ponytail. I knew there were tribes with goblins in the jungle, but I'd never seen one up close.

"I don't want to hurt you," I said, showing the goblin both of my hands.

"Promise?" They managed to say through tears.

"Promise," I agreed. I placed one of my palms on my chest and held the other facing the Goblin. This was the symbol of swearing an oath of our goddess, Estel. I know the goblins in the jungle worshiped the same goddess and I hoped they had similar traditions. The Goblin mimicked my motions and touched their palm to mine. Their face began to relax a bit.

"I'm Karuk," I introduced myself. "What are you doing all alone in the city?"

I knew Goblins had similar rules to Orcs. They also only entered the city in groups.

"You won't tell?" they asked. I couldn't help it, I let out a laugh. "What? What's so funny?" they asked.

"Who would I tell?" I asked. "We're here by ourselves."

"Oh, right," they remembered. "My name is Gin. I snuck into the city."

I was impressed that it would even occur to a Goblin this young to sneak into the city. I wouldn't have dared to come here by myself. I was too afraid of what would happen. It must have shown on my face because Gin's mouth crept into a grin.

"You don't think I'm crazy?" he asked.

"No. Well, maybe a little," I admitted. " But I'm mostly curious. Why would you want to come here by yourself?"

"The music," he said simply.

"What music?" I inquired.

"I heard Goblins talking about how people played music in taverns. I love to play music with my tribe, but I get tired of the same thing all the time. I wanted to hear something new," Gin explained.

I never really cared for the music of my people, so I couldn't understand risking my life to hear a new song. But I could relate to getting tired of what life in the jungle had to offer. I basically had two options. I could be a hunter, like my father, and join the hunting parties. Or I could become a domestic worker, like my mother. I could stay at the settlement and process the animal pelts, cook the food, and prepare for religious ceremonies. All my life, I knew that doing one of those two things would be my destiny. I couldn't help but wonder if there could be a third option. I never dared speak it, because I worried the tribe would think I was ungrateful. But, still, I wondered.

"I get it," I empathized.

"Really? You'll help me?" Gin said, presuming I already understood what exactly he was asking of me. I considered the look of excitement on his face and I couldn't stand to be the reason it faltered.

"Sure," I agreed. "Let's go listen to some music."

"Woohoo!" he exclaimed, jumping into the air and revealing the small drum slung across his body. I quickly ran to look down the road, making sure no one heard. It looked like we were safe.

"Try to keep it down," I whispered. "If we're going to travel through the city, we can't let any adults see us. They'd probably arrest us, or kill us, or something."

"I know," Gin said meekly. "Sorry."

"You can be excited," I advised. "Just do it quietly."

"Woohoo!" he whispered, slightly raising his fist into the air.

"That's better." I said with a slight giggle in my voice.

"So where are we going?".

"To a tavern, to listen to music. Didn't I tell you that?" he asked

"I know that, Gin. Where is the tavern?" I asked.

"Oh, I don't know. We have to find it," he said, as though it was the easiest thing in the world.

"You mean I'll have to find it," I said, reaffirming what he meant.

"Yeah, what'd I say?" he asked.

"O.K.," I said. "I think I might know where to start."

I led Gin down the way I'd come and walked over to the open lot where I saw Pyson and Tini playing earlier.

"You came back to play with us!" Tini exclaimed upon seeing me.

"Not right now," I explained. "My friend and I were actually looking for a tavern. Do you know where one is?"

"I do! My mommy took me to one a few days ago for breakfast. We had eggs with cheese and bacon. It was really good!" she said.

"Do you know if they play music there?" Gin asked.

"I think so. There was a big stringed instrument on a stage. It was bigger than me!" Tini said.

"Bigger than me?" Pyson asked curiously.

"A little bit," Tini said.

"That's funny," Pyson replied, laughing.

"It is!" Tini said, joining in his laughing fit.

Gin and I started laughing too. I didn't fully understand why, but it was fun. We calmed down about a few seconds later.

"So you know how to get there?" I asked.

"Yes!" Tini said defiantly. "You go down that way one block, then you turn right and walk for three blocks, then you turn right again and walk two blocks."

"Thank you!" I said.

"You're welcome. What are your names?" Tini asked.

"I'm Karuk," I said. She grabbed my hand and started shaking it.

Pyson picked up Gin and held his little Goblin body even with his face.

"And you are?" he asked.

"I'm Gin," he said as the giant pulled him in for a bear hug.

"See you later!" Tini said, waving her arm above her head. Pyson gently set Gin down and did the same.

"Bye!" Gin said as I began pulling him down the street.

We followed Tini's directions, and I was heartened to see the sun was beginning to set. We'd be a lot harder to notice as an Orc and a Goblin without the sun shining down on us. I kept us close to the buildings, and we moved at a slow pace so we wouldn't draw attention. Tini's directions weren't perfect, but I could tell we were getting close when we started to hear music ahead of us.

"That's it!" Gin excitedly whispered. He tugged on me to pull me down the street. He headed for the front door, and I pulled him past it.

"What are you doing? It's right there!" Gin complained.

"We can't just walk through the front door. We'll get caught!" I reiterated.

Gin looked annoyed, but he understood. We walked around to the other side of the building and saw an open window around the back. There weren't any doors on this side and it faced the wall between the city and the jungle.

"Hey! This is close to the hole I snuck through!" Gin exclaimed.

"Good, we can sneak out after we listen for a bit," I said.

We sat down under the window and leaned against the building. As the music drifted through the window, Gin looked like the happiest person I'd ever seen in my life. He tapped out a rhythm on the edge of his drum. It wasn't too loud, but he got to feel like he was playing along.

I didn't expect to get anything out of this. As I said, music has never really been my thing. But then I started listening to the lyrics. They were singing songs about people going on adventures. There was a song about a woman who had been kidnapped by a Troll and she fought her way out. Another song told of a human man and a Gnome woman that traveled through the hells and outsmarted a Demon lord to save their village. Then my mind was completely blown when I heard a song about an Orc woman named Tadarin who had rushed through the barrier between Anglachel and "The Jungle of Despair," which I guess is what they call the jungle here. Anyway, she ran through the barrier and single-handedly battled a Dragon that had swooped down to attack the city. They considered her a hero! An Orc hero!

After we finished listening to the musicians for the night, I walked with Gin to the hole he'd snuck through and helped him through it. We promised to meet up at a clearing between our settlements next week to sneak in and listen to music again. I crept along the edge of the wall until I spotted the guards at the gate into the jungle. I'd gotten there right in time. I could see my father talking to a guard. I figured he was asking about me. I slipped around the street and joined the other Orcs in the back of the hunting party. I could hear what my father was saying now.

"We just want to look around for her a little bit longer. Could you just let the town guards know what we're doing?" he asked tentatively.

"I'm sorry, sir," the guard said, hand on the hilt of his sword. "We can't let Orcs remain in the city at night. That's the law."

I walked up to my father and tugged on his fur cloak. He looked down and a huge grin spread across his face."Karuk! You're here!" he exclaimed.

"I was in the back," I lied.

"We're good sir," he said, turning back to the guard. "We can leave now."

"Thank you," the guard said, relieved. "I'm sure neither of us wanted any trouble."

I crossed through the gate with the hunting party, thinking about the songs I'd heard that evening. For the first time, I started to feel like I knew what I wanted to do when I grew up. I wanted to be an adventurer.

Don't Call It That

"**P**raise to Estel, the great goddess of balance. She, who uprooted the evils away from our lands and gave our people the ability to thrive." The large fire in the center of the tent flared as the old Shaman threw powder into it. They waved their spiritual stick above their head, dried jungle fruits hanging off of it. They were human with long gray hair, and skin the color of a mountain range at sunset. The Hukawan tribe, a collection of humans and Orcs, gathered in the large ceremonial tent in the center of the village at the ending of every week.

"Praise to the trees, the soil and the animals that sustain us. Praise to the balance of nature that allows all creatures to live alongside one another," they continued.

I stood up with the rest of my tribe as we began to wave our hands above our heads. I've started every day just like this for as long as I can remember. I was nineteen years old at the time and I appreciated being a part of something bigger than myself, but I also wanted more than the life the tribe could provide. I wanted to be like Tadarin and all the other heroes Gin and I had heard about for the past three years. I was beginning to grow tired of preserving my culture in exchange for never leaving. I needed to get out.

"What do you mean, you want to leave?" my mother incredulously asked the first time I'd brought it up just after that first encounter with Gin.

"I just don't know if I want to be a hunter or a domestic tribesman for the rest of my life. What if I want to live in Anglachel, and just work an office job or something?" I sheepishly asked.

"Karuk, my dear girl, you are an Orc of the Hukawan tribe. Who would hire you in Anglachel? You know that they are scared of us," she concluded.

Sadly, I knew she was right. I always saw the way the people of the city looked at us. I knew there was no place for me in the city.

But that doesn't mean I didn't crave it. I found myself feeling envious of the human children born in our tribe. They had options that simply were not available to me.

After the morning ceremony, I hid within the crowd so I could sneak out of the village without my family noticing. Once I made it into the open jungle, I raced through the trees, jumping over roots and swinging across branches. Some of my earliest memories were racing against adult hunters across the jungle. I always had a knack for finding my way through the wilds. I noticed the way this branch curved upward, or how those roots spread out a little farther. I may have wanted to leave the tribe, but I still loved the jungle.

I made it to a clearing beside the large waterfall. I'd been coming here for the past three years and it was the only place I could drop my mask and fantasize about the life I truly wanted. This was the place I could truly be myself.

I heard Gin approach before I saw him. His drumbeat carried throughout the trees and I could hear the birds singing along. He danced his way into the clearing, lost in the music. Gin's thin, muscular arms beat a rhythm more appropriate in an Anglachel tavern than in the middle of the Jungle. His yellow-green skin, the color of an unripened lime, shone in the sunlight. Sweat dripped off of his pointed nose and ears. As he finished his song, I offered a hearty applause.

"Stop it, stop it," Gin said. "It is only us here. You can just say thank you for the private concert. You know, I should charge you for this."

"Of course," I replied, grinning at him, "What sort of game would you like for payment? Boars seem to be plentiful this time of year."

He gave me an unsatisfied look.

"Oh, you wanted coin?" I asked sarcastically. "I'm afraid an Orc of the Hukawan tribe has no use for it."

Gin unstrapped the drum from his shoulder and collapsed into a nearby moss pile. "I know that's not true."

I followed his lead and sat on a log from a recently fallen tree. "Maybe so, but where would I get it?"

"I keep telling you, Ruki. We need to go to the city. I could play at a tavern and earn us some money. You know I'm good enough," Gin said.

"You're no doubt good enough. I've never seen anyone so skilled with an instrument that they can call upon magic without a ritual," I said. "But how would we get past the guards? They would never let either of us enter the city alone, much less together. The only way an Orc or a Goblin can get into the city is with a trade party. And there's no way we could sneak away without getting ourselves killed."

"You can stop being practical any time now," Gin begged.

"It is a nice fantasy," I offered.

"It is that."

I swung my legs onto the log and began to lay down. Just as I started to lounge, I heard the scream. A distinctly masculine voice from somewhere down the river. I launched out of my seated position to grab a vine hanging from the trees above. I scrambled up the vine so I could get a better view of whoever it was from above.

I squinted my eyes to better focus in the distance. I could see a river boat, clearly of Anglachelan make, careening towards the waterfall at an accelerating speed.

As it got closer, I could see a panicky, tall, young human. He had shoulder-length, unkempt chestnut-blonde hair, and wore a long black trench coat. He was running from one side of the boat to the other. He screamed again, and this time I could just make out what he was saying.

"Help! Someone, please! Help me!"

I lept into action, making my way down to the river by swinging from alternating vines. I couldn't dive in. His boat was too big, and if I was to have any chance at stopping it, I had to use the leverage of standing on the ground provided. But his boat was too far out for me to reach him.

"Quick, give me a platform," I called out to Gin.

He sprung up and threw his drum around his shoulder in a singular motion. He quickly began beating out a driving rhythm. A solid pink force field appeared, jutting out of the river bank. I easily lowered myself onto the force field and it began to blink out. I had to jump to avoid crashing into the rapid river. The force field reappeared as I came back down.

"Sorry about that," Gin wailed, "I've never had to use these for anything practical before."

"You're fine, just try to keep it steady," I instructed.

Now that the surface began to feel a bit more sturdy, I drew my hunting ax from my belt. I had constructed it from my tribe's ancestral steel trees—the strongest wood that I knew of. As long as I could keep hold of it, it wouldn't break. As the boat raced past, I thrust my ax into it. It was a solid swing and it stuck. It tugged hard on me, but I was able to ground myself on the pink force field. I slowly walked it back to the river bank.

The human ran to the back side of the boat and shouted, "Ve Ex To!"

The river still beat against the boat, but the pull decreased. I eased it to a stop, getting off of the pink force field; the human and I took a deep breath. His golden rectangular glasses fogged a bit.

"Thank you, thank you so much!" he said, lifting his head. A startled look appeared on his face as it tilted towards us.

"Don't worry," I assured, "Neither of us intends to hurt you. That would have been a lot of effort to save someone just so we could kill them."

That didn't reassure him.

"Not that that's the only reason we wouldn't kill you. Goblins and Orcs aren't actually as aggressive as everyone says," Gin continued. "I'm Gin. This is Karuk. Her friends call her Ruki."

That seemed to do the trick. The young man began to ease his shoulders a bit.

"They do not," I whirled on Gin. "You're the only person that calls me that, and you can only get away with it because we've been friends for so long."

A smile began to creep onto the human's face.

"M-my name is Dara," the human piped up. "Dara MacCarthy."

"Nice to meet you," I returned. I extended my hand towards him and realized I hadn't sheathed my hunting ax. I quickly tucked it back into my belt. Gin had sauntered up and offered his hand before Dara could notice my mistake.

"You as well," Dara said. "Sorry if I was impolite earlier. I was just surprised to see an Orc and a Goblin together. I had always heard that your tribes hated each other."

"No, we like each other," Gin replied.

"I'd more say 'tolerate,'" I explained. "My tribe, the Hukawan, stay on this side of this river. Gin's tribe stays on the other side. In the centuries our tribes existed, we found it works better for everyone. There's always enough resources to share."

Dara nodded, as if he was considering this. "That makes sense."

"And we're not all Orcs. The Hukawan are both Orcs and humans," I said.

"Yeah, yeah, yeah," Gin interrupted. "And Goblins live with Halflings. Everyone knows that. You don't need to bore our new friend to death already."

Dara gave a light laugh.

"She does this," Gin stage whispered to him.

"No, no, it is fine," Dara stated. "It is actually exciting to learn something new. I don't think it is common knowledge in Anglachel that there are indigenous humans and Halflings in the Jungle of Despair."

"Please don't call it that," I corrected. "We let you people say that because it keeps you all out. But we just call it The Jungle."

"Of course, of course," Dara apologized. "I'm so sorry."

I didn't want to scare him, but it was admittedly humorous to trip him up socially. "You're good."

"So what brings a scrawny human like you out into The Jungle?" Gin asked.

"It's like I said. I wanted to learn something new. I was a student at Arcana University and I felt like I had learned everything they had to teach me. I thought I'd strike out on my own into The Jungle. My boat got out of control when I tried to tap into the potent elemental magic here."

"That checks out," I said. "Our shaman has said that the magic is nearly uncontrollable here. But we don't know anything about the different flavors of magic. Is that what you call them?"

"Disciplines, but yes. I have actually never seen anyone tap into barrier magic the way you did, Gin. What kind of training do you have?" Dara inquired.

"I wouldn't say I have training. I've just always been really tuned into music and anytime I play I've been able to create pink force fields. I don't know what that is," Gin admitted.

"That sounds similar to sorcerers, people that are born with the ability to tap into a specific discipline of magic. But I've never seen it require music. I would be very interested to study that," Dara suggested.

"Sure."

While they were talking I took a moment to assess our surroundings to make sure we were safe. The reason Gin and I liked meeting here is that it is a pretty open area with fewer trees than the rest of the jungle. While we're here, most of the animals stay away because they don't want to be spotted. All I could hear were the sounds of the babbling river and insects buzzing around.

"So you were just planning on living in the Jungle?" Gin asked.

"Oh no, not at all. I want to travel the world. I actually have a checklist of all of the different geographic regions in Galevyn," Dara excitedly explained.

I turned around at the mention of a new word. "Galevyn?"

"That is what we call the planet we live on, in Anglachel. And in the rest of the world, as far as I knew," Dara said quizzically.

"Really? We always just called it 'Earth.' Because, ya' know, dirt," Gin responded.

Dara reached into a bag hanging off of his shoulder and pulled out a quill and a small notebook. He whispered something into the feather and began scribbling something down. "Wow," Dara exclaimed. "I guess it is a totally different world out here. So exciting!"

We stood there in awkward silence for a moment, looking at each other. I don't think we knew what we were supposed to do next. Gin and I have never spoken to a magic student before. Dara had surely not spoken to an Orc or a Goblin before.

"So you said you wanted to travel?" Gin finally asked.

"Yes," Dara said. "Once I get my boat to the sea, I can use some minor transmutation magic to turn it into something that can get me across it."Dara paused and considered his beached boat on the river bank."But I don't know how I'll get it there," he said, seemingly noticing for the first time. "I guess I have to go back to town already. Everyone's going to make fun of me."

This sounded a little bit like an adventure and maybe an opportunity for Gin and I to start figuring a path out of The Jungle.

"I could help," I chimed in.

"Yeah?" Dara asked. "You'd do that for a person you just met? That's so nice."

"I never said I was doing anything for free," I said directly, folding my arms.

"My coin is pretty limited," he began.

"No, don't pay in coin!" Gin said. I glared at him. What was he doing? We needed this coin to get out. "You can pay us by letting us go with you!"

"That's fine with me," Dara said. "After seeing the two of you handle yourselves earlier, you could be very useful to have around."

"One moment," I interjected. I grabbed Gin by his arm and dragged him far enough to be out of Dara's earshot.

"What are you talking about?" I demanded. "We can't just go. We have to plan. We have to pack. We haven't even said goodbye to our families."

"Do you really think your mom or dad will just let you go if you told them? I don't know about your tribe, but I've heard stories of Goblins thrown in cages by their brethren because they were saying crazy things like going into the city alone."

"No, I have heard those, too. Our people's position with the city is so precarious, they can't risk anyone messing everything up," I remembered.

"Yeah, that's right," Gin smugly said. "How many chances are we going to get like this? A magic human showed up, WITH a friggin' boat? I've got my drum, you have your ax. We have everything we need. How is that not a sign? We have to go with him."

I considered his words for a moment. I'd spent my whole life praising Estel, the goddess of balance. In a way, this may be the only way Gin and I could get away from our tribes. After two centuries of Orcs and Goblins being stuck in this jungle, maybe this is tipping the balance for our people. Even if only slightly.

And Gin is right. As much as I want to say goodbye to my tribe, my parents, they'd never understand and they wouldn't just let me go. If we really wanted to leave The Jungle, really leave, this might be our only chance. I looked back towards my village before deciding.

After a beat, I dragged Gin back to Dara.

"I can walk, ya' know," Gin complained.

I looked Dara in the eyes. "We will go with you."

"Cool!" Dara said. "So are you going to carry this boat by yourself or . . . ."

"I can handle one side. The two of you are going to have to try to hold the other side up so it doesn't drag," I instructed.

"I'm a musician, Ruki," Gin said. "I don't really do manual labor."

"What am I getting myself into?" I asked myself aloud as I picked up the front end of the boat.

Swimming Through the Storm

We had only just started drifting into the open sea when the storm became a problem. It doesn't often storm in The Jungle, but when it does, it pours. And apparently, the weather gets way more extreme out on the sea. It became very clear to me very quickly that Dara had no idea how to captain a ship, let alone steer it in these conditions. It was all we could do to stay afloat and on the deck.

"Any ideas, wizard man?" Gin screamed over the sheets of rain.

Dara struggled as the boat shook in the waves. "Hold out until morning and then find our bearings?"

"You want us to keep fighting this storm all night without knowing if we're even making any progress?" I questioned. Judging by the looks on Gin and Dara's faces, they knew I had no intention of doing that.

Dara held his hand over his face to block out the rain and looked up. "If I could see the stars, I could figure out what way is south. But I can't see anything through these clouds."

"I'll figure it out." I decided, after considering our situation and realizing that something had to change if we were going to make it. Gin and I were not going to run away from our families just to die out here.

I dove off the boat and into the sea. I could hear shouts from Gin and Dara, but they didn't matter right now. I knew that we were never going to figure out what direction to head from out here, but I knew that I could always find my way around The Jungle. The shoreline hadn't quite faded from view yet, and I furiously swam towards it. It wasn't easy swimming through the storm, but my Orcish body was built for this kind of thing. I just kept going until I reached land. I don't know how long it actually took, but every muscle in my body was screaming.

My hand finally landed on a muddy patch at the bottom of a plateau facing the sea. I remembered passing it when we had started the journey. I began climbing the rock face and pushed the pain into the back of my mind. I didn't have time to worry about that right now. I just kept pulling myself up the shale until I reached the top.

Once there, I surveyed my surroundings. I used to come out to this cliff to watch the ocean after a long day of hunting. I saw the pair of trees that led to the deer trail I could follow to the outskirts of my settlement. I mentally followed the trail and considered where the settlement would be in relation to this cliff. I pointed my palm straight in front of me and traced where I would be. When I ended at the edge of my home, my hand was facing sharply to the left of where I'd started. I knew the settlement was due north of the river we'd taken to reach the sea.

I kept my hand where it was, and I turned my head to see the boat. I could see them in the distance, a speck, but a speck that was clearly facing in a north western direction. If we traveled that way all night, we'd probably end back up on the opposite side of The Jungle. That wouldn't be helpful. We would have to adjust the boat about 120 degrees east to travel to the south. I looked around to see if there was anything on the jungle floor I could use once I'd made it back. I spotted a thick, long vine. I sliced about four squares of it with my hand ax and wrapped it around my shoulder like a sash, tying it in front. Then I took a deep breath and dove back into the water.

I was once again swimming through the storm, but I kept my eyes on the speck of a boat I saw in the distance. It gradually became bigger and bigger; then, finally, I could hear welcoming shouts from my compatriots.

"Ruki!" Gin exclaimed. "You're back!" Then he slapped me across the face as I was climbing back onto the boat. It didn't hurt, he's a little guy, after all. "Never do that again. I'm not doing this without you. We never leave each other."

I toppled onto the deck, but I looked Gin in the eyes.

"Sorry, Gin, you're right. We never leave each other," I agreed.

"Why did you do that?" Dara asked. "What were you trying to do?"

"I figured out which way we need to go," I stated matter-of-factly.

I pulled myself up, and I gestured in the direction we needed to turn the vessel.

"I'm impressed," Dara said instinctively. "That was insane. But I'm impressed."

"Is there a way to block the wind so we can try to, I don't know, paddle that way?" I asked both of them.

"I could play a barrier around the sails," Gin suggested.

"And I can create wind. If we can block out the other wind, I can produce wind in whatever direction we need to go," Dara said.

"You're gonna have to help me, Ruki," Gin said, looking at me with pleading eyes. "It is real hard to play in this storm."

"I know what to do," I concluded.

I unlashed the vine from around my shoulder, and I tied it around Gin's waist. I pulled it taut and braced myself to keep him in place. Dara positioned himself directly behind the sail, and Gin began to beat a rhythm into his drum. A sort of pink tent appeared, protecting Dara and the sails from the surrounding storm. I could see he was reciting something, but I couldn't hear it through the whipping winds around us. He pulled a modest candle from his coat, produced a tiny flame on the end of his index finger, and lit the wick. He closed his eyes and held his hand in a southerly direction. He blew out the candle, and the boat jerked, fighting against the waves to move us closer to either Ronan or Ferreria, the countries across the sea to the south of The Jungle. We didn't know where we were headed, but we had absolutely begun our lives as adventurers. Gin continued to play his drum but looked at me with a huge smile on his face. I returned it. It was really happening.

Following the Dirt Road

We ended up on a pebble beach on the northern shore of Ronan. Past the beach, we could see rolling green hills extending into the distance. Growing up in The Jungle, the amount of open land was shocking. It felt unnatural to see so much green space without trees around.

"So what now?" Gin asked.

We all looked at each other expectantly. The ten seconds that followed felt like ten minutes.

Gin looked at both of us incredulously. "Really? No one has thought about the next part?"

"I don't know if you noticed, but we were all a little busy keeping the boat afloat to consider next steps," I reminded him.

"Come on, Ruki," Gin pleaded. "We've been thinking of this day our whole lives! You've gotta have some idea of what you visualized. After we left home to become adventurers, we . . . ." He paused expectantly.

"Why are you looking at me? You were there, too," I argued.

"Don't do this, Ruki. Don't you start blaming me," Gin preemptively defended.

I've always loved Gin. That charming Goblin kept me sane through most of my childhood, but sometimes childhood friends know exactly how to push your buttons. I was tired, I was lost in a new place, and Gin was getting on my last nerve. I could feel myself breathing heavily and I'm sure my face looked as mad as I felt.

"O.K., O.K.," Dara mediated. "Guys, we just landed. We're exhausted. Let's try to find a town and rest. I still have a little coin to get us a room and a meal at a tavern."

"That's it, a tavern!" Gin remembered excitedly. "I can play there for extra money, and we can find adventuring work!"

"That sounds like a plan," I groggily concurred. "And I didn't even have to come up with it. Should we just start walking until we find a road?"

"Yeah, shouldn't take long," Dara responded. "I've read that Ronan is known to have many small villages scattered throughout it. One writer joked that you can't throw a rock without hitting one."

Gin picked up a pebble from the beach and chucked it. Gin is lean and muscular, but it's all for aesthetics. He is not built for strength. The pebble landed among its rocky compatriots further down the beach. "False," Gin declared.

I rolled my eyes. "Just start walking."

It turns out Dara was right. Once we reached the top of the first grassy hill, we saw a dirt road below. I took a moment to appreciate the view. There was a sea of green as far as the eye could see. It was stunning. We turned right on the long stretch of road and walked for about twenty minutes. We eventually saw a wooden sign emblazoned with bright red lettering that read, "Welcome to Éindí Grá!"

Éindí Grá, I would come to find out in the coming weeks, was a typical quaint Ronan village. The dirt road continued into the town and ran down the length of it. We saw a provision store, a doctor's office, a number of small houses, and a tavern. The tavern in this town was called Cabbage and Ale, as evidenced by the hand-painted wooden sign that featured a tankard of ale beside a steaming bowl. My tribe occasionally traded for ale, but I had never actually eaten cabbage before. It must not be native to the jungle.

"Ruki! It's really happening!" Gin excitedly said to me. His delight eroded some of of my weariness away.

"We're becoming adventurers!" I agreed, and a smile crept onto my face. The reality of our dreams coming true was too thrilling to deny.

I noticed Dara had been nervously twirling a gold coin between his fingers. "I just hope they accept Anglachelan gold."

The streets were pretty barren, it felt a little like a ghost town. I was basing that entirely on descriptions I had heard of ghost towns in tavern songs. But there were signs of life. There were large buckets with ladles hanging from a rope that occupied the porches of a number of houses. Fruit pies were sitting on windowsills to cool.

We entered the Cabbage and Ale, and I was struck with a whiff of home. In our settlement, the most prominent smell was always the burnt smell that came with the large fire we used to cook group meals. I was starting to regret leaving without telling anyone goodbye. The Cabbage and Ale featured a prominent fireplace in the center of its modest dining room.

"Give us a moment," a heavily accented matronly voice called our way. "We're only just gettin' past our lunch rush. Have yeself a seat and we'll be with ye shortly."

A chubby Gnome woman with a thicket of reddish-gray curls on top of her head stood behind the bar. The bar top was surprisingly short, though that made perfect sense when considering the size of the proprietor. The majority of the tables were also the same kind of compact, but there were a couple of medium-sized tables near the back corner of the establishment. Dara, Gin, and I seated ourselves as the Gnome woman walked into a room behind the bar. We sat quietly and took in the comfortable, inviting space around us.

A moment later, a much younger Gnome woman came out of a back room. She carried a stool in one hand and a notepad in the other. She was presumably some kind of related to the first woman, based on their similar facial features. Conversely, her curls flowed onto both of her shoulders in a waterfall of vibrant red. She wore a white collared tunic sloppily tucked into her form-fitting leather pants. She placed the stool in front of our table and stepped onto it with the precision of someone who had been doing this for most of their life.

"Mam said there was some tall folk here," she began.

"Yes, we were wondering. Where is everyone? The streets are empty," Dara asked.

The girl laughed to herself "Oh, you lot must not be farmers. They're all working the fields. That's what ye do in the mornin'."

That made a lot of sense. We had farmland in The Jungle, but I was always a hunter. Gathering crops was never one of my responsibilities. I could remember when I was very young, and I'd see my mother walking into the settlement with a basket full of vegetables and herbs. I put my elbow on the table and rested my head on my hand. I didn't want anyone to see the tears that had started to well up at the thought of home.

"What can I get ye?"

"What would someone so beautiful as yourself recommend?" Gin asked in a flirtatious tone.

"Oh, I didn see ye back there," she laughed. "So ye guys have a lil' one with you, too. I thought ye were a child or somethin'."

That properly took the wind out of Gin's sails. A grin crept onto my face, realizing how nice it was to see someone else deflate him.

"Don't mind my friend," I apologized. "We would appreciate a recommendation though. We're not from around here."

"Oh, ye don't have to tell me," she responded. "We don't get many

Orcs or Goblins around these parts. Our special is the stew bubblin' over the fire. That's never a bad choice."

"Then give us three of those," Dara answered. "And some water would be great."

"I'll get ye guys some ale," the waitress said.

Gin and I hadn't been to anything even slightly resembling a restaurant, so we were grateful that Dara had ordered for us. The stew was like nothing I had ever tasted before. The broth was a deep brown color and very salty. There were chunks of tender meat that weren't like the game I had eaten back in the jungle. It was also loaded with vegetables. There was a pale green, leafy vegetable that I gathered was Cabbage and Ale's namesake. There were also carrots, potatoes, and fibrous tiny green half-moons. It was delicious, or at least it was so different from anything I had ever eaten before that my brain processed it as delicious. While we ate, we began discussing our next moves.

"So, what do you guys want to do?" Dara asked.

In hindsight, it was surprising that Dara hadn't thought any of this through. He must have wanted to get away from wherever he was coming from as much as we did.

"I want to play here!" Gin exclaimed. "I bet these Ronan Gnomes know how to get down!"

"I meant how do we want to find our first adventure," Dara clarified.

I glanced around the tavern and didn't see any jobs posted. All the songs said that adventurers got jobs from a wanted board. I was confused.

"I thought there were supposed to be jobs posted somewhere in here."

"That's more for big cities," Dara explained. "In small towns like this, everyone basically already knows what's going on. If someone needs help, they just ask their neighbor."

"Just like back home, Ruki," Gin said. "I guess other people aren't that different."

I hated when he got overly saccharine. "Yeah, very sweet, I guess. But that doesn't help us now. We want to be adventurers! We have to have something to do for it to count as an adventure."

"Maybe somewhere around here there's someone who needs help and would be willing to pay?" Dara suggested.

"I've got it!" Gin said, jumping onto his seat. His small Goblin legs standing on the chair brought us face-to-face. "I'll play here tonight, then you guys can ask around with the huge crowd I'll bring in."

"I don't know if we can count on that," I began.

"That's right, Ruki! It is a great idea!" Gin agreed with the version of me he had conjured in his head.

"Is he o.k.?" Dara asked.

"Yeah, you'll get used to it. Sometimes Gin gets an idea and nothing we say can pull it out of there. He just has to do it. It looks like we're waiting until nightfall," I said, accepting our fate.

"That's fine," Dara said. "We need to rest anyway. I'll get us a couple of rooms."

There was only one room available at the Cabbage and Ale. Apparently, it was some sort of Gnomish holiday and a lot of people were in visiting family. To be honest, I had always thought that when Gin and I made our great escape, I'd never look back. I had spent years accepting that I would never see my tribe again. It was comforting to realize that other cultures left home and came back for visits. That sounded nice.

Gods, I needed to shake this homesickness. Why couldn't I just enjoy doing the thing I've always wanted to do?

Our room was Gnome-sized, so Dara and I let Gin have the bed. We both curled up on opposite sides of the room.

"Ruki," I heard his whisper from the bed.

"I'm trying to sleep, Gin," I complained.

"I just wanted to say, that I'm glad we could do this together. I talk a big game, but I would have never had the nerve to leave without you. Thanks for sticking by the weird Goblin that wanted to play music."

While he was being very sweet, it was also undeniably sappy. I would usually call him out for it, but I let him have this one.

"Thanks for sticking by the Orc who wanted to be a hero. I'm glad you're here, too," I said.

"Gods, Ruki, don't be such a sap," Gin teased.

I don't know how long we slept, but the window outside looked very dark by the time we began to stir. I was awoken by Gin springing out of bed and forgetting that I was sleeping beside it on the floor. It didn't hurt, he was so small, after all, but before I could say anything he was already bolting for the door.

"Where's the fire?" I sleepily asked him.

"I don't want to miss the crowd," he said quickly. "This is my first time playing in a real tavern. I don't want to mess it up!"

He ran out the door and closed it behind him. I looked to the other side of the room, and it looked like Dara was in a similar state.

He blearily opened his eyes. "Was that Gin?"

"Yeah, he's chasing his dreams," I yawned.

"Good for him," Dara said. "Do we have to get up and go watch him?"

"Have you never had friends before?" I laughed.

That brought a smile to his face. "Is that a real question? I'm a dorky wizard, of course, I didn't have friends."

"Aren't most wizards dorky?"

"Much to my surprise, they are not. I was hoping I'd find my people at Arcana University, but it was just a different kind of cool kid that excluded me."

I started pushing myself off the floor. "I know we've only known you a couple of days, but I'm pretty sure you found your people. Let's go support Gin."

We took our time getting ready and washing up in the water basin in our room. When we opened the door, I heard a completely different atmosphere than the one we'd walked into. There was a cacophony of voices coming out of the dining room. Dara and I walked out and stood out like sore thumbs. The place was packed with Gnomess. They all were about waist high on the two of us. I felt like a Giant. I spotted Gin, it wasn't hard from way up here. He was frantically talking to the old lady who was the proprietor of this establishment. I tried to walk over to him without literally stepping over the other customers. That felt rude somehow.

"Please! This is the first real tavern I've ever been to. I need to play!" Gin said when I caught up to him.

"If you must," the elderly Gnome relented. "But you better be good. Your room will cost you more if you run these folks out."

"I don't think you have to worry," Gin confidently replied, winking at the woman as he walked away. Was he flirting with this old woman? Gods, I hope this doesn't become a thing with him now that we've left The Jungle.

Dara had claimed the "tall folk" table that we had sat in earlier. I gladly joined him. I was not about to continue towering over these Gnomes. Gin found an open corner on the opposite side of the tavern. He began beating a driving rhythm on his drum. I saw dozens of red-colored heads turn in his direction.

"Hello everyone, my name is Gin," he shouted over his playing. "Are you all ready to have a good time tonight?"

The crowd erupted in applause. I had never seen my friend happier. Suddenly all of my concerns faded away. This was the right choice.

The Gnomish crowd loved Gin's music. That was a relief. I always appreciated his talent, but the only real audience he had played for was his Goblin tribe, and from what I hear, that didn't go well. His catchy beats may not suit his kinsman, but they were perfect for these Gnomes tearing up the dance floor.

"Do ye need anything?" The young waitress from before said. She had snuck up on us, or it was just crowded, and we didn't notice.

"I'm good for now," I replied.

"You love him, don't ye?" she asked.

I felt my cheeks turning red, and I felt flustered."No. Dara and I have just met. We're not together," I said.

"I meant the Goblin. Ye keep staring at him with that dumb smile on your face," she clarified.

I let out a big belly laugh."No, Gin is like my brother. I'm just happy for him. He has dreamed of playing in a tavern his whole life," I explained.

"That's sweet," she said. "What do ye want?"

"I want to travel and have adventurers," I said.

"A woman after me own heart," she said. "Once mam can find someone to work the tavern, I'm plannin' to get out of here."

"I wouldn't mind the company," I said. Was I flirting now? Is that what flirting feels like? I was always so focused on finding a way out that I never really explored any kind of a romantic relationship back home. Most people in my tribe stay together for life. Why lead someone on when I always planned on leaving?

"Ye wouldn't, would you? I wouldn't mind traveling with a big, strong woman like yeself. Ye're quite the looker, too," she complimented.

I was glad I wasn't drinking anything because I definitely would have spit it out. I did not expect this Gnome woman to find me attractive. I can't imagine she sees many Orcs in this small town.

"I'm Tilly," she offered.

"Karuk," I managed to get out.

"Well, Karuk, I hope you'll look me up before leavin' town. Maybe we can get to know each other a little better," she said with a wink. She walked away to find other customers.

I was relieved when I looked beside me and saw that Dara had left. It was a bit less embarrassing that no one I knew saw my first ever attempt at flirty banter.

Dara plopped back into the seat beside me. "I've found us a job!"

"Yeah? What are we doing?"

"Apparently, Old Man O'Reilly has been having some trouble with his beag sheep. He's been losing a couple every few days."

"Lost sheep? That doesn't exactly feel like an adventure," I complained.

"Begging adventurers can't be choosy adventurers," Dara said. "And who knows, maybe some sort of monster is eating them or something. There could be some action."

I relented and agreed to take the job. At least it was something.

Because we'd slept through the day, I wasn't really tired. Dara, Gin, and I ended up gathered around the table at the end of the night.

"It was amazing!" Gin beamed. "It was everything I'd ever dreamed of. They loved it, I loved it. I could do this forever!"

Dara patted him on the back. "That's great, Gin!"

"It was incredible to see other people into your music. You were definitely in your element," I observed.

"I really thought I was going to regret leaving in such a rush, but gods, this is the best!" Gin confessed.

The homesick feeling that had been nagging with me finally boiled over. I couldn't hold it in any longer. "I miss everyone," I blurted out.

Dara looked completely confused, like he didn't know what to do. Gin swiftly crawled across the table and jumped into my lap to give me a hug.

"It's o.k. Ruki! We're going to be heroes."

"I know. I'm glad we're doing it, but I can't believe I didn't tell anyone goodbye. I want to travel all over Galevyn, but The Jungle will always be my home." I used the fur shirt on Gin's shoulder to wipe my tears.

"We'll probably go back before you know it," Gin tried to reassure me.

I knew that his heart was in the right place, but my head wasn't hearing any of it. "But how long will that take? We barely even have money. We're gathering sheep tomorrow. We could be stuck here forever!"

"You can send a message," Dara said.

"What?" Gin and I said simultaneously.

"I'm a wizard, aren't I? I know a little bit of divination magic. We could send a message to your family."

"But I can't do magic. The shaman in my tribe tried to get me to do it when I was little and I was no good at it," I admitted.

"I can do all the hard parts, you just have to visualize the person you want to talk to and say the message," Dara explained.

I felt myself calming down a bit. "I think I can do that."

"See, Ruki! You're back before you know it, like I said. Well, your voice will be back, because of magic or something," Gin stumbled.

Dara explained that I was going to be the one to cast the spell ultimately, but he was going to write a scroll that could contain the spell. He pulled a blank scroll and his magic quill back out of his bag. He also pulled out a much smaller feather and a bottle of rosewater. He spent about ten minutes drawing an elaborate magic circle on the scrolls, featuring overlapping circles, triangles, and random scribbles I didn't recognize. He put the small feather in the center of the scroll, dipped his finger in the rose water, and traced the circle with the rosewater. He closed his eyes and grabbed the feather by its base with the tips of his fingers. He then yanked the feather out of the circle and it flashed a green light.

Dara opened his eyes and he was overcome with a wave of lethargy. "It's done."

"Are you o.k.?" Gin asked.

"Yeah, yeah," Dara reassured us. "Putting spells onto paper just takes a lot more out of me."

It meant a lot that he went through that for me. "Thank you."

"No problem. Honestly, it's nice to be able to do magic for people that appreciate it." Dara laughed. "All you've gotta do is place one hand on the scroll and the other hand on your head."

He demonstrated without actually touching the scroll.

"Then you just have to picture the person in your head and speak the message out loud. If they reply, you'll just hear it in your head. I'm going to go to bed now," Dara finished.

"You're the best, buddy!" Gin complimented.

Dara grinned at that. He's found his people.

I did as Dara instructed and I pictured my father in my head. I took a deep breath. "Dad? It's me, Karuk. I left The Jungle. I made a couple of friends and we're going to become adventurers. I know you don't understand. I don't expect you to. But I want you and mom to know I love you. I appreciate all you've done. I'll be home soon, once I become a hero."

It didn't take long for a reply to come. "Karuk? We were wondering where you were, but we weren't worried. We knew you could take care of yourself. Me and your mom knew this day would come. I'm glad you're making friends, you always had trouble doing that with the tribe. We love you. Take care of yourself."

I began to cry again, this time tears of joy. Gin had scooted a chair super close to mine while I was doing the ritual. He hugged me again.

"Did it work?" he asked.

"Yeah," I replied. "Yeah, it worked."

*****

Dara, Gin, and I headed over to Old Man O'Reilly's field the following morning. He had a cozy farmhouse and a large, fenced pasture where the beag sheep grazed. I had never seen beag sheep before, but they were probably the cutest animals I have ever seen, and I'm not one to typically discuss the cuteness of animals. Beag sheep appeared to be like any other sheep, but were smaller and pastel-colored. That explained all of the pastel-colored clothing that most of the Gnomes wore.

Dara suggested we walk the perimeter of the fence for clues. The fence looked like it had been smashed in on one far end of the field, very far away from the farmhouse.

"Think this is our culprit?" Gin asked. "The sheep are just walking out and not coming back?"

I walked up to the broken wood.

"This looks like it's been smashed. Maybe there is a monster involved." I really didn't know much about what sort of monsters lived in Ronan, but I had images of a manticore; a lion with Dragon's wings and a scorpion tail. Or a chimera, a creature with three heads, one each of a lion, goat, and Dragon, and its tail is a snake. Those were two of my favorites from the songs. I didn't dare dream I might get to fight a Dragon, like Tadarin, or drake, which is like a smaller dragon.

Dara walked up to join me and closely examined the broken fence.

"I don't think it's a monster," Dara began.

"Dammit," I said.

He crouched down and touched the broken ends of the fence. "But we may still end up fighting something. These cuts are clean. Someone cut this fence to look like it had been smashed. Someone is framing a monster. We've got ourselves a livestock thief on our hands."

"Woohoo! This is getting interesting!" Gin exclaimed.

After Dara discovered that a person had abducted the beag sheep, our next steps seemed pretty obvious.

"So, we just want to follow whatever trail there is to find the missing sheep?" I asked.

"I don't think there's a trail, Karuk," Dara observed.

"Yeah, this break in the fence is the only thing here," Gin agreed.

It was almost cute how little they both knew about tracking. I grew up in a hunting tribe in the jungles of Anglachel. I don't care who took these sheep, there was some sort of trail.

"I can track them."

"Are we sure we just want to go straight to the sheep? Don't we want to figure out who took the sheep?" Dara questioned. "When we thought it was a monster, the motive was sustenance. But why would someone try to make it look like a monster took them?"

"You're thinking about this too much," I complained.

"He might have a point, Ruki," Gin joined in. "This person's motive might tell us how dangerous they are. Maybe we don't have to go climbing all over the hills of Ronan if this person is still in town."

I decided to humor him. "Let's pretend like that's the best idea. Where would we even start?"

"We'd have to investigate," Dara began. "We would need to talk to people in town and see if there is anyone that had ever expressed any ill will towards Old Man O'Reilly."

"That sounds dumb. We're just going to follow the trail," I decided. I walked through the hole in the fence and began looking for clues. I wasn't sure if they were going to follow me, but after my abrupt dive off the boat, they knew that if I thought I had the best path forward, I wasn't going to be stopped. I heard voices in the background, but I blocked them out because I was already in tracking mode.

Whoever had taken these sheep was pretty good at covering their trail. There really wasn't much left. But they weren't good enough to fool me. While this person was obviously treading lightly and trying not to leave any evidence, sheep are going to do what sheep are going to do. The most obvious sign of movement was the subtle trail left by the beag sheep in the grass. Admittedly, it was reassuring that the sheep were walking themselves. They could still be alive if this person hadn't decided to kill them right away or load them up in some sort of vehicle. It also meant they probably weren't very far away. As I continued following the trail, I could hear footsteps behind me. I was glad Gin and Dara had come to their senses.

The hoof tracks led us to a rockier set of hills near the beach. The trail became slightly harder to follow, because the sheep wouldn't leave much of an indention in stone, but it looked like our culprit had traveled this way many times. There were signs of well-worn hand and foot holes along the hillside. This person had been climbing to avoid leaving much of a foot trail. That was smart. Most people wouldn't look along the steeper parts of the hill for clues.

"Are we going to be there soon?" Gin whined.

"I don't know, Gin. I didn't make this trail," I reminded him.

Gin sighed. "I know, but did they leave any sign that they're close to where they brought the sheep? My sandals were not made to climb rocky hills like this."

"What do you expect? A note that says, 'stolen sheep pen just ahead?'" I sarcastically asked.

"Probably not?" Gin said skeptically. "Or did they? Is this a trick to embarrass me?”

“You can’t be serious.” I laughed. “No, Gin, they didn’t leave a note or any other sign that we’re getting close. This person is actually pretty good. They’ve been trying to hide their tracks.”

“Should we be worried?” Dara asked.

“I don’t think so. So far, all the signs I’ve seen belong to one person and a small group of sheep. I think this person is working alone.”

“That’s reassuring,” Dara said. “I don’t know if we could fight a bunch of people.”

“Don’t worry, I’ll protect both of you. No matter what we run into, I’ve got you,” I said.

Dara’s face relaxed in relief. “I’m glad.”

We continued up the rocky hill for about thirty more minutes. We had to double back a couple of times because they had left false trails. Eventually, we ended up at the opening of a cave. We also began to hear bleating sounds.

“Is that the sheep? That sounds like the sheep,” Gin inquired.

"I think so, but we don't know what sort of stuff we're going to encounter in there. Both of you stay behind me," I instructed them.

We eased into the cave and it was very dark. My Orcish heritage allowed me to see in pretty dark areas, but I couldn't see much in the way of details. With that being said, I did spot a pile of way too extravagant pillows for a cave along the right wall. I drew my hand ax just in case we ran into any trouble. I began to approach it. I saw something squirming and a tiny pair of wings.

"What is that?" I thought aloud.

Before I could stop him, Dara walked past me to approach the pillows.

"I think that's a . . . Ah!" he exclaimed. Gin and I also yelped a bit.

Dara had triggered a net trap. As we began to be suspended in the air, I lost my grip and my ax clattered to the ground below. A rope net tightened around us and we all became much closer than we had been the previous night in the single room.

"Baby gwiber," Dara finished. "I think that's a baby gwiber. It is a snake with wings. I don't remember reading about them being native to Ronan. That little guy is pretty far from home."

"Fascinatin'," Gin flatly commented. "Do you think you could get your elbow out of my crotch?"

Dara frantically and apologetically readjusted himself, which only made the whole situation more uncomfortable for the rest of us. The net began swinging dangerously.

"Could we stop moving?" I asked in a way that sounded more like a command. "None of us like this. We have to figure a way out. Dara, could you burn us out?"

"I don't think so," Dara observed. "This is a little too tight for me to cast my spells. I have to gesture and I can't really do that here."

"O.K. Gin, can you play your drum to conjure a barrier to cut us out?"

"You really think I can beat on a drum with your ass shoved up against it?" he grumbled.

Then it was up to me. I began staring at the rope to see if there was a weak spot I could push to break it. This all would have been easier if I hadn't dropped my hand ax. This was a mess of a first adventure.

"What're you lot doing here?" A female voice called from the mouth of the cave. I looked over and saw a bundle of curls atop a backlit short silhouette. I recognized the voice.

"Tilly?" I questioned the figure.

"And of course you recognize me. I didn't want to kill you. I was hoping I could clear this place out before you placed me. Oh well," she conceded, drawing a dagger from her side that shone in the sunlight.

"Kill us?" Gin worriedly screamed.

Tilly chucked a dagger in our direction and I managed to jump a bit, causing the net to bounce up as the dagger swung in our direction. I timed it just right so it would slice through one of the bottom ropes. As the net swung back down, I pushed myself feet first through the newly formed hole. I landed and scooped my hand ax up in a single motion.

"You're not killing anybody today," I replied, taking a defensive position.

"That was all very cool, Ruki," Gin said. "But do you think you could help us down? Not all of us are as athletic as you and it is taking everything I've got to hold onto these ropes."

I looked up and saw Dara and Gin clinging to the rope net so they wouldn't crash into the cave floor beneath. But I couldn't focus on them right now.

"Hang on a bit longer," I advised and rushed up to Tilly.

"Whoa, whoa, whoa," Dara shouted across the cave. "Nobody has to kill anyone. Tilly, was it? Why do you think you have to kill us?"

"Ye're adventurers, aren't ye?" she said. "You're going to want to kill my baby over there. That's what adventurers do, right? KIll rare creatures?"

"You must have heard some nasty rumors," Gin reassured. "Or we don't know as much about adventuring as we thought. We don't want to kill anything unless we have to."

"Truly?" Tilly asked.

"Yes," I shouted, trying to tamp down the adrenaline coursing through my veins. Tilly lowered her dagger.

I used the moment to help Gin and Dara down from the net. Then if she decided to turn on us again, at least we'd all be able to fight. Once we dusted off our clothes and took a moment to stretch a bit, Dara began to walk towards her slowly.

"What is a baby gwiber doing here?" he asked. "I thought they were native to Daragon."

"I don't know, I just found her one day. A big egg washed up on the beach and wings hatched out of it. I've been takin' care of her ever since. I didn't tell anybody because I know how my community reacts to anything weird or dangerous," Tilly explained.

"That's why you needed the beag sheep," Dara concluded.

"Yeah, she needed more meat than I could swipe from the kitchen at the Ale and Cabbage. Stealing sheep seemed like my best option."

"We can help you get her somewhere safe," Dara said.

"Really? Where? Do you want to take her to Daragon?" Tilly asked.

"We don't need to go that far," he explained. "I've know about a magical creature reserve across the mountains in Reyes."

"Would all of you really want to help me after I tried to kill you? Well, at least strongly considered it."

"Do you promise not to try to kill us again?" Gin asked.

Tilly paused like she was thinking about it. "Sure."

Gin chuckled at the bit. "Then we're good."

I wasn't so sure, but I felt confident that I could watch our backs around her and keep us safe, now that I had some sense of what she could do.

"If the two of you are good with it, I'll let her come," I said.

"We should probably just leave," Tilly said. "I don't want to explain this to my mam."

"No," I remembered how much I missed my tribe when I left without saying goodbye. "We're going back and you're going to explain it to her. I'll go with you, but you're going to tell her."

"And I left my backup components in my room there anyway," Dara said.

"Ruki," Gin said.

"Yeah," I replied, looking down at him.

"Saving a magical creature and traveling across a continent feels like a proper adventure," he said.

"That it does," I agreed. I reached down and put my hand on his shoulder. He placed his hand on mine. And that's the story of how Gin and I became adventurers.

I'm Sure It's Fine

We headed back to the Cabbage and Ale to speak with Tilly's grandmother. Once we explained to her that Tilly had found a baby flying snake called a gwiber and that we needed to take it to a magical creature reserve to keep it safe, she was surprisingly accommodating.

"I knew this day would come," she said, nodding while her graying reddish curls gently bounced on her head.

Tilly cocked her head in confusion. "Mam, you always talked to me about how I would take over the Cabbage and Ale one day. Why would you do that if you knew I was going to leave?"

"You will learn one day. It is a grandmother's job to make their grandchild feel guilty about leaving. I just wanted to make sure you knew what ye were leavin',” she said.

She helped Tilly pack and even gave us a map to help us cross the mountains. Gin, Dara, and I stood outside the tavern while Tilly finished her goodbyes. Watching her hug her grandma warmed my heart. I was glad we could make sure Tilly's grandma got more than I left my family. Tilly bounded in our direction, cradling the gwiber.

“Are we doin' this?” she asked.

“You betcha!” Gin exclaimed. “Do we just hike up the mountains like we did when we tracked your cave?”

“According to this map, we have two options,” Dara began. “We can try to find a passageway under the mountains, or climb over them.”

“Under sounds easier,” I offered.

“It does,” Dara agreed. “But my Dwarvish isn't the best. I don't know if I could talk our way in.”

“I know a bit,” Tilly said. “Every now and then, the Dwarves come to the Cabbage and Ale between expeditions. They're pretty into my grandma's cookin'.”

"That sounds promising!" Gin yelled.

"Sure, between the two of us, we should be able to figure something out," Dara agreed.

We followed the dirt road out of town and stopped at the base of the mountains, where the road just sort of abruptly ended. Tilly told us that some of the traders use goats to cross the mountains, but they just pack everything on the goats and ride straight up the cliffside.

"The map says the entrance to the Dwarven part of Ferreria is to the north of this road," Dara explained. "It looks like the door should be marked with a symbol of a triangular science beaker."

"What's a science beaker?" Gin asked, and I was glad because I had the same question. We studied nature and learned new things in The Jungle, but we didn't use science in the way Anglachellean society thinks of it. Mercifully, Dara just showed us the picture instead of trying to explain all of the science to us.

"Why would they use a beaker for their symbol? Everything I have ever read about Dwarves referred to them as miners," Dara inquired.

"That's actually a nasty stereotype," Tilly stated. "They do mine. Most of the dwarves that swung by the C&A did a lot of mining, but they did it to study the rocks. It's not about gettin' it, it's about studying it."

Dara's face lit up at learning something new. "Fascinating."

We walked up and down the edge of the mountain range, closely inspecting every odd-looking group of rock formations. If there were doors there, they were awfully well hidden.

Finally, Tilly started peering down an opening between two different outcroppings of rocks.

"I think I got somethin'!" She had since handed the gwiber-sitting duty off to Gin, who was having an absolute blast trying to teach the flying snake to flap its wings to the beat of his drum. Tilly used her small Gnomish frame to climb through a small opening in the rocks and was standing inside a tiny overhang.

"I don't think this is right, Tilly," I said. I still didn't fully trust this girl, and her instincts certainly weren't going to be what I trusted first. "Aren't Dwarves a lot stouter than you? They wouldn't be able to squeeze in there as you did."

"Of course not," Tilly shrugged off. "They must have some science-y doohickey that opens it for 'em."

I approached the outcropping and started inspecting the rock cage that Tilly was now standing inside. They looked like normal rocks. There didn't appear to be a seam or anything that showed a place the rocks would move into to open it up for a Dwarf-sized user. But Tilly was convinced; I could see in the columns of light peeking through the rocks' openings that she was fiddling with something inside.

"I'm coming inside," I announced.

"How? You can't fit!" Tilly complained.

"I'll just bust through the rocks. I can't let you be in there by yourself. You might get hurt," I said, trying to explain why I needed to keep watch on her.

"Or you think I'll leave you three behind," Tilly said, accurately accusing me. "Don't forget, your Goblin friend has the gwiber. I wouldn't leave him behind."

She was right, but I still wanted in there to ensure she wasn't making us wait around while she poked at some random rocks before realizing it wasn't an entrance to Ferreria. I pulled my hand ax out of its sheath and started tapping away at the rocks at the top of the entrance.

"Watch it, Orc girl! You might trigger somethin'," Tilly whined.

"I'm sure it's fine," I assured her.

I successfully chipped one rock column away when I felt the ground shake under my feet. I could tell by the unchanging expressions of Gin and Dara that it was only just happening where Tilly and I were standing.

Tilly looked smug, she seemed to be enjoying this. "I told you."

Abruptly, the ground beneath Tilly and I slid away. We fell into the darkness below.

The fall happened fast. Usually, time kind of slows down when you have a dramatic fall, but when you're falling in complete darkness, I guess your brain can't really process what's happening. As we were falling, I needed to position Tilly on top of me. I knew that my Orcish frame could handle the fall much better than her tiny Gnomish one.

"What are you doin?!" Tilly yelled at me when I put my hand on her to usher her in my direction.

"Trying to save your life!' I screamed back, continuing to pull her.

"Who said I need saving?!"

"No one needed to say it! We're falling down a dark pit, I have no idea what's at the bottom. Your little body won't be able to take the fall the way I can."

"I can see down there, it looks like just flat stone," she said as I smashed into it. It definitely stung, but I'd spread my body out enough to even out the impact across it. Tilly scrambled off of me as my eyes began to adjust to the darkness. She began examining the wall.

"Are you guys o.k.?" Gin's voice emanated from the hole at the top.

"I'll live," I responded.

"Do you see a way out? Maybe a button or an emergency ladder?" Dara asked.

"No, it looks like a sheer rock wall the whole way," Tilly shouted up.

"We'll figure something out," Dara said, less reassuringly than I'm sure he intended. "Maybe I can figure something out with Gin's barrier magic."

"Sounds good," I said. "I could use a few minutes to rest."

Tilly turned in my direction and rushed to my leg. My head followed her, and I could see what had worried her. My leg was covered in blood. I felt pain there, but it wasn't any worse than the pain running through the rest of my body from the fall.

"Karuk! You have to let me patch you up!" she said urgently.

"Go ahead," I relented. "I"m not exactly in a position to stop you."

Tilly pulled out a candle and lit it. She lifted my leg and examined it all over.

"It looks like it's just a really bad scrape. You should be fine, but I need to clean you up and cover it, so it doesn't get infected."

"How do you know first aid?"

"I was always an accident-prone child, and my grandma taught me what she was doing every time she took care of me."

"I never needed to know that kind of thing. My tribe doesn't let us travel alone if they can help; we always have a healer with each group. That allowed people like me to focus on hunting," I said.

"I get that," she said. "But if we're going to be traveling together, you really should learn a bit of first aid yourself. Someone needs to be able to put me back together if I go down."

"I wouldn't let any of you get hurt," I said, a bit surprised that I'd actually meant it.

"And how is that working out for you?" Tilly asked as she pulled a flask out of her belt and twisted the cap off it. She poured the brown liquid on my open wound.

"Ahhhh!" I wailed.

"That's what I thought." This girl loved being right.

"Hey, that's cheating!" I retorted.

"There is no cheating in love and war." She laughed.

"And which one is this?" I asked. "We weren't really fighting anyone when we fell."

"Working with you feels like a bit of both," Tilly said thoughtfully.

"I'm not always like this," I said apologetically. "I just don't trust easily. It is hard to forget you trapping us in that net and talking about killing us."

"You don't need to apologize," Tilly said. "I get it; I'd feel the same way. And honestly, I don't want you to change around me. I kind of like feeling the thrill of worrying that you're either going to punch me or kiss me."

"That doesn't sound healthy," I jested. "I'd only punch you if you deserved it."

"Don't you kink-shame me!" Tilly joked back. "I'm just tryin' to tell you that I like you the way you are."

That did something to me. I never felt like I fit in with my tribe. They were all about preserving the jungle, and they would never have understood how much I wanted to see the world. I knew Gin cared about me, but I always worried he was just putting up with me because we were the only ones that understood each other. Tilly telling me she liked me the way I am was something new. I felt something warm on my cheeks.

"Thank you," I managed to get out.

"Don't mention it. Don't go getting mushy on me, we've got a lot of land to travel before we deliver the gwiber."

"Right," I replied.

The room began to brighten as a pink spiral staircase began crawling down the walls of the hole.

"Is that you, Gin?" I yelled up.

"He can't really talk," Dara shouted back down. "He has to concentrate and play really softly."

"He must hate that," I yelled back up.

"Shut up, Ruki!" Gin screamed quickly.

The pink staircase stuttered out of existence for a second.

"Maybe don't bother him right now," Tilly suggested.

"Yeah, you're probably right," I said, chuckling.

"Race you up the stairs?" Tilly challenged.

"You're on," I said, rushing in front of her to be the first to start climbing.

Passing Through Montläken

I t took us a while, but we eventually found an entrance into the Dwarven settlements under the mountains. After we found the trapped door, identifying another set of rocks that were a bit off-color from the rest of the mountain was just a matter of finding it. I let Tilly do her thing this time, and she was able to get us in. The first set of Dwarf guards we ran into were hesitant about letting us in, but Gin was able to talk them into it. Part of me thinks the novelty of seeing an Orc and a Goblin was enough to get us through.

Before long, we found ourselves in the massive Dwarven city of Montläken. The city was completely under the mountain, but you wouldn't know it from where we were standing. The stone around the city had been carved into a smooth dome that extended into the air for what looked like nearly 3,000 squares. Standing at the entrance, I could have thought I was looking at Anglachel were it not for the tunnels that dotted the streets. There was an earthy smell that filled the air.

"What do you think those are?" I asked Dara, gesturing to one of the tunnels.

"They must be mining tunnels. It is simply fascinating that they treat these tunnels the way we treat any other kind of infrastructure in Anglachel," Dara beamed.

It made sense. The sound of explosions, likely creating new mines, were nearly constant.

"It's where they all work, it's got to be part of the city," Tilly reasoned.

"So what do we do now?" Gin asked. "Just walk through the city and find a way out on the other side?"

Dara shrugged. "That's as good a suggestion as anything I could come up with."

We entered the city limits, and Montläken only grew more impressive.

The buildings appeared to be carved out of the same stone as the ground. They'd literally carved their buildings out of the mountain instead of constructing them. I couldn't even begin to fathom the amount of forethought that planning this city would have taken. This would have been enough to blow my mind fully, but then I noticed the fine detail carved into each building. They'd carved all of this by hand! I would have been willing to bet they'd used magic to dig out this place.

We had only begun admiring the city whenever we were stopped by the local guards.

"Grüezi," one of the guards said, speaking in Dwarven.

Tilly uttered a couple of things back and forth with him until she eventually turned to us and said, "They said they'll take us to the King. They said he'll probably want to meet us anyway, and he can speak North Elven like you."

"Should that worry us?" I asked. I didn't know much about Dwarven culture, but I did know that being escorted to the leader of a nation immediately after entering didn't seem like the most normal thing to happen.

"Nah," Tilly replied. "In my experience, Dwarves work hard, but they're mostly friendly. Brusque but friendly."

I wasn't entirely convinced, but I was trying to start trusting Tilly. I kept my apprehension to myself and followed. We were led around a large, central lake to a towering castle with pyramid-shaped roofs topping the different towers. It also appeared to be carved directly out of the mountain. Flags were flying on the rooftops. They showed the same image of the science beaker Dara had shown us before we entered. I guess doing science really is what they prioritize.

We were led through a long hallway until we finally made it to a huge set of doors.

"King in there," one of the guards said in broken North Elven.

I looked around, and my party looked pretty apprehensive. They were definitely feeling the same way as me. I knew one of us had to be brave, and since I'd already shoved my doubts into the back of my mind, it was up to me. I walked up to the door and pushed it open. I could feel my friends following at my heels. The throne room was modest in comparison to the rest of the city. It was large enough to hold twenty or so people at most. Directly in front of us was a set of five steps that led to the throne. The steps and the throne were connected with the floor. There was an intimidating Dwarven figure sitting on it. He sat stoically, so I continued to walk forward.

I didn't know enough about Dwarven culture to know who this person was. Obviously, he was a king since the guards said so, but was he the king of the entire Dwarven nation of Ferreira? Or was he just the king of Montläken? Did Dwarves even consider themselves part of one nation? I was starting to wonder why we even agreed to come here.

"Do my eyes deceive me, or do I see an Orc, a human, a Gnome, and a Goblin? What a curious party to pass through Montläken," the king said with a bright yet gravelly voice. His face was covered with a bushy beard, but the top of it seemed to rise, indicating he was smiling.

"Yes, sir," I began. "We were hoping to pass through Montläken in order to reach Reyes."

"Would it be safe to presume you are a group of adventurers then?" the king asked.

"Yes! We definitely are!" Gin said excitedly. "What gave it away? Is it because we look so cool and strong?"

"Something like that," the king said, a slight giggle in his voice. This was going better than I thought. He at least seemed happy to see us. "I will grant you passage," he stated. "But I need you to do something for me in return."

"Anything," Tilly immediately responded.

"The tunnels we use to mine obsidian have been challenging to access for the past month. It has greatly set us back on our research," the king explained.

"So you need us to do the research?" Dara asked hopefully.

"I'm sure you are smart," the king said. "But I was hoping you could provide a more violent solution."

"We can do violent!" Gin exclaimed. "Ruki here is an incredible fighter!"

"Good, good. The tunnel has been infested with imps. You see, if we dig deep enough, our tunnels tap into The Hells. Nasty things sometimes find their way in. Our researchers aren't equipped for combat, and our guards are really mostly for ceremonial purposes. You would be doing us a great favor if you could clear out the imps. If you could find a way to stop them from entering, that would be even better. Follow the tunnel, it will eventually lead you to the city of Valnan. Valnan will have an entrance to Reyes. Bring back something unique from the tunnel that we haven't studied yet, and I'm certain the King of Valnan will reward you handsomely."

"Awesome!" Gin said. "We're in!"

*****

The imps infesting the Dwarve's obsidian tunnel were actually pretty easy to take out. They were essentially bats with tiny humanoid bodies and heads. As far as I could tell, they weren't sentient, just wild animals. The tunnel itself was well lit with glass tubes affixed to either side. The glass tubes shined with a dull orange light, similar to candlelight but more consistent. Occasionally, the tunnel got dark because the imps had smashed up the magic lights. Dara was able to quickly conjure a bit of light that we could fight by. I know that we had figured out what was happening to Old Man O'Reilly's beag sheep and we are currently helping Tilly get her baby gwiber to Daragon, but slaying these things felt like our first real adventure. Striking down demonic vermin was the kind of thing me and Gin would talk about doing.

Eventually, we came to a fork in the tunnel. The magic lights had been busted up on both sides of the fork and it wasn't clear which was the right way to go. There was broken glass on either side.

"Which way?" Gin asked the group.

Dara started rummaging in his bag. "Gimme a sec, I'm going to see what I can find out."

He pulled out a crystal and tightened his fist around it. He closed his eyes and reached out his hand, moving it around like a dowsing rod. He did this for a couple of minutes until his eyes snapped back open and he faced us again.

"It's weird," he began. "Both sides show powerful magic."

"Maybe both ways lead to Valnan," Tilly suggested. "It is the next city along this path."

Dara pursed his lips in thought. "I don't think so."

"What is it?" I asked.

"It's just. . . this side feels like identification and transmutation magic," he said, pointing down the right path. "This way feels like destruction and elemental magic."

"You're the only one here that has any idea what any of this means, buddy," Gin urged him. "Why don't you just tell us what you're thinking."

"The Dwarves worship the goddess Lovelace. She rules over identification and destruction magic," Dara explained.

"Identification sounds more like Dwarves," Tilly suggested. "They're all about research and stuff."

"That's my first instinct too. But they could be using destruction to carve out new tunnels. It really could be either side."

"What do we have to worry about if we get it wrong?" I asked him.

"Well, these imps have to be coming from somewhere. I've never read anything that says where The Hells are, but it makes as much sense as anything else that they could be way underground," Dara reasoned.

"So we either make it to the city or we go to hell?" Gin asked.

"Pretty much," Dara confirmed.

I put my hand on his shoulder. "Do we want to reason this or do you just want to decide? We trust you either way."

"Elemental sounds like demons and devils, ya' know, fire and stuff," Dara said. "But we know for sure that the Dwarves use elemental magic, that's what all these lights have been conjured from. And it frankly feels more like them to use destruction magic to build with than transmutation. They carved that whole dome and their buildings from the same stone and the extra had to go somewhere, unless it didn't. Destruction magic fully destroys the matter it is used on and converts it to magical energy. To me, that makes more sense than them using transmutation magic. It would just turn the stone into something else."

"So head towards destruction?" Gin asked.

Dara was having trouble trusting himself. His eyes were darting back and forth. "I think so."

I still didn't like not being sure. I knew what I had to do. "O.K., just wait here, guys. I'll sneak ahead since I can see in the dark."

"Hold on, Karuk!" Tilly interjected. "I can see in the dark, too. I'm coming with you."

My mouth instinctively lifted into a grin. I looked to the ground to hide it. "O.K."

We crept into the darkness, walking silently for about five minutes. After Tilly admitted she liked me in the hole trap, I felt awkward whenever it was just the two of us.

"So Dara is pretty impressive," Tilly whispered, just loud enough that I could hear her, but no more.

I was a little worried that my voice wouldn't get that soft and I'd give us away. "Yeah, it seems like he can do pretty much anything with magic."

"I was pretty sure that people could only ever do one discipline of magic at a time, but he's done both divination and elemental just in this tunnel."

I knew a little bit about magic, but not enough to keep a conversation going. We walked in silence for a bit longer. I should say something. I looked around for something to talk about."This mine tunnel is really smooth."Gods, why did I say that? Who cares about the the roughness or smoothness of rock?

"Yeah, it must be destruction magic, like Dara said. It's weird, right?" she responded.

Whew, she thought it was interesting. What now? Should I compliment her?"Your hair is curly."

"Yes, Karuk. Are we just saying things we see now?"

Dammit. How did I think that was a compliment? I spotted wings flapping towards us in the distance."Imp ahead," I warned.

Tilly drew her dagger and took a fighting position. I drew my ax. The flapping got close enough that we could hear it. I charged towards the imp. I was running faster than I had before and I lost my footing, tumbling to the ground.

"Karuk!" Tilly yelled, as she rushed towards me and the imp. She jumped and used the wall for leverage to jump again. The dagger slashed through the imp and two wings clattered to the ground. I could now see that what we thought was an imp was actually a bat. I rolled over and laughed.

"What?" Tilly looked offended. "Did I do something weird? Was my form off?"

"No," I managed between laughs. "We were scared of a bat!"

"Oh my gods, really?" Tilly asked. She picked up one of the wings and joined in my laughter. "Sorry, pal."She fell down on top of me. Her small body felt warm in the cool mine air.

"Me too," I said.

"You too what?" Tilly asked.

"I like you, too."

*****

We rejoined Gin and Dara and after a very long walk in near darkness, we began to see light at the end of the tunnel. It was a bright, white light, similar to what it looked like when we left Montläken. There were a pair of Dwarven guards standing on the other side of the well-lit hole.

"What are you doing there?" a gruff feminine voice asked. Their armor made them indistinguishable. It seemed like, at least among the guards, Dwarves didn't care about gender. I appreciated that.

"We've been sent here on a mission from the King of Montläken!" Gin exclaimed.

"Are you telling me you four took care of the imps in this tunnel?" the other guard asked.

"You know it! Don't you ever forget that the Misfits of Fortune did that for you!" Gin said.

"What did you just call us?" I asked.

Gin puffed his chest out. He had clearly considered this moment. "Our name. The Misfits of Fortune! It sounds like something that would be sung about, right?"

"I mean, sure," I said. "We can workshop it later." I turned my attention back to the guards. "The King of Montläken said we should talk to your King."

"Oh yes, I'm sure he'll want to reward you," the Dwarven woman said.

"Shit!" Tilly cursed.

"What is it?" I asked.

"I forgot about finding something rare," she explained.

"Is this anything?" Gin said, holding up a hard gemstone, colored in a swirl pattern of amber and obsidian.

Dara's eyes widened. "Gin! That's concentrated transmutation magic!"

"So, it's something?" he asked hopefully.

"It's really rare. It is definitely something," Dara said.

"Yay! We did it!" Gin shouted in celebration.

Just Get Over Here

After weeks of travel under the mountains, through Dwarven and Devil territory, we'd finally made it to Reyes. The exit out of Valnan opened into a narrow rockface along the ocean. We had to carefully skirt across it until we'd reached the broader side of the mountain. The Dwarves of Ferrerira really knew how to hide their settlements. The mountain was covered in grass and opened into a large field. It was wild to think that less than a month ago, I'd never traveled beyond Anglachel. Gin and I were really, truly adventurers.

There weren't any obvious roads, but Dara was able to send another message using divination magic to one of his former classmates from Arcana University who was finishing up his practicum at the magical creature reserve we were headed towards. He instructed Dara to wait next to the mountain, and he would come to pick us up.

"What do you think he'll pick us up with?" Gin excitedly asked. "Maybe a Dragon with a broken wing? Or a herd of alaricorns? Oh, Oh! What if it's a panther!"

"Don't even joke about that," Dara snapped.

"What? I don't know anything about panthers. Are they scary or something?" Gin asked.

"Your tribe must have similar stories to mine," I said. As far as I knew, no one had actually seen a panther. At least, no one had seen one and lived to talk about it. They were the sort of things the older folks would scare kids with. "If you don't eat your vegetables, the panther will come to get you!" That sort of thing.

"Sure, I've heard the stories," Gin answered. "But we're adventures now! Don't you want to see one for yourself? They might not be so scary."

"All I ever learned about panthers at Arcana University is that you don't want to run into one. The textbooks describe them as 'cat-like,' but that's all it ever says. I would like to see one, but there is no way we're ready to fight one yet," Dara explained.

Tilly threw her arm around Gin's shoulders. "Let the little guy have his fun. It's not like you say the word 'panther' and one appears."

"You're right," Dara said apologetically. "Sorry I snapped at you, Gin."

"You're good, buddy. You're probably right. We'll see a panther one day, but we probably shouldn't see one today," Gin agreed.

Before we could move on to another topic, we saw something bounding toward us from across the field.

Dara pointed to the figure in the distance. "This is probably him now."

The approaching mass looked small at first, but as it got closer, we could tell this was a massive creature. It looked sort of similar to a boar, but it had a much larger nose and different coloring. The creature had white stripes along its side, like a skunk, but with many more stripes. It galloped in our direction like a horse. A Human man rode atop it.

"Dara! Don't tell me you made friends!" the man yelled in our direction.

"Reggie! How are you?" Dara tried shouting over the pounding hooves.

The large creature came to a stop about two squares away from us.

Reggie tossed one leg over the animal and slid down its flank. He tossed a feather in the air before he landed and it slowed his descent. As he landed, he walked in our direction.

"Sorry, I didn't catch that," Reggie said. He had tan skin and dark, tousled hair. The kind of hair that looked intentionally messy, but would probably take all morning to get to look that way. The mud on his work pants and thick button-up shirt indicated that it actually just fell that way naturally on his head. It was infuriating.

"I said that it's been forever, Reggie! How are you?" Dara said, offering his hand to Reggie. He took it and pulled Dara into a deep hug.

"I'm doing great, buddy. I'm loving it out here. But it is great to see a familiar face. There's no one around here that looks like me," he confided.

"That must be hard," Gin said facetiously since we'd been the only Orc and Goblin around ever since we'd started our journey. Reggie didn't seem to get it.

"It really has," Reggie agreed. "But I can't believe that little Dara has made a friend, much less three of them. Are you doing an adventuring practicum?"

"Something like that," Dara said, lowering his head to look at the ground.

"No, we are adventurers!" Gin interjected. "We just fought some imps under these mountains!"

Reggie let out a long whistle. "Traveling through the Hells. Dean Constance must have it out for you."

"Yeah," Dara said, looking off into the distance. He started scratching the back of his neck.

"So what is this thing?" Tilly said, mercifully changing the subject.

Reggie gestured towards the boar creature. "Oh, this little feller? This is a Giant Tapir. This one's just a baby, you can tell from the stripes along its side. The adults have solid-colored flanks."

"That's a baby? It is enormous! How big are the adults?" I said, trying to keep us on this topic a bit longer. I was also genuinely curious. This "baby" was as tall as a large tree in the jungle.

"This guy's about finished growing. He's just not lost his stripes. We took him in because we found him about a mile outside of the reserve without a mama. We presumed poachers hunted her. They get some good money from their pelts," Reggie said. He was clearly in his element talking about these creatures. "You said in your message you had something for me?"

"Yea," Tilly answered. She took the backpack-bed we'd fashioned to keep the gwiber in. The winged snake began to stir and poked its head out of the bag.

"Oh my goodness," Reggie exclaimed. "What a cutie!"

"I found her just outside of my village. I'm from Éindí Grá," Tilly elaborated.

"What would a gwiber be doing in Ronan? They usually aren't found outside of Daragon," Reggie asked himself.

"We were hoping you might be able to tell us," Dara said. "Or at least be able to take her off our hands."

"Yeah, sure," Reggie agreed. "I'm sure my boss would love to have one of these in the reserve. Arcana University provides funding for each magical creature we house."

"And she'll be safe?" Tilly asked.

"Couldn't be safer," Reggie assured her. "If there's anywhere that will make sure she grows up happy, it's here."

I visibly saw Tilly take a sigh of relief.

"Shall we?" Reggie offered, gesturing towards the Giant Tabir.

"Definitely!" Gin cried out.

Once we got to the animal reserve, Dara had to go make arrangements with Reggie and his boss. Gin offered to take care of the gwiber until they returned. I think he'd grown attached to the little thing. That left me and Tilly waiting by ourselves on the edge of the reserve. We sat on a fence surrounding a herd of Beag Sheep. It was interesting that we were ending our time together around the animals that first brought us together.

Tilly looked out at the rising and falling mountains in the distance. They were covered in green, with the occasional brown spot, where the mountain shifted into rock. The closest had a waterfall running down it. "It's beautiful here,"

"Yeah," I agreed. "Are you going to be o.k. making it back home? Do you want us to go with you?"

"You worried about me, big girl?" Tilly teased.

"We came this far together. It seems wrong to leave you behind."

"I agree. It seems a shame to leave us behind," Tilly replied.

"You have become one of us. The team could use someone like you if you'd want to stick around," I said. I lifted my arm to brush my hair out of my face, but really I was covering up the crimson that was surely spreading across my cheeks.

"Really, Karuk? The team wants me to stick around?" Tilly laughed. "You're going to have to do me one better than that."

"I wouldn't mind if you stuck around either." I turned my head, finally looking down at her. She had been staring at me, and our eyes met.

"Why don't you just say that you like me? Do you want me to say it? I like you, Karuk. I want to travel with you to see if this is anything."

I felt something in my stomach I'd never felt before. Like a flock of birds were flapping away down there. I squatted down to make our faces even.

"Do you care if I—" "I began.

"Just get over here," Tilly interrupted, pulling my face to hers. Her lips were soft but demanding. She kept pulling me in for more. Her hand ran through my hair, and I placed my hand on her back and pulled her deeper into the kiss. I didn't know how much time passed.

It could have been minutes, it could have been an hour. Finally, we pulled apart and looked each other in the eyes again.

"That'll do, Ruki," Tilly said, smirking.

"I told you only Gin gets to call me that," I chided.

"We'll see. I want to check on my girl before we leave her behind. Race you to Gin?" Tilly asked.

"As if you even had to ask," I said, sprinting past her.

"That's cheating, Ruki!" she said, chasing after me.

The Magic Animal Reserve

Gin

This place is incredible! I have spent my life in the jungle feeling like I'd seen every plant and animal there was to see, but here I am surrounded by hundreds I'd never even heard of. I mean, I'd never even heard of a gwiber, and now I've been traveling with Gintina for weeks now. I've named the gwiber Gintina, by the way. She kept looking at me with her cute beady eyes like she wanted a name so I decided to give her one.

Dara went to talk with Reggie about making arrangements for Gintina's new home and Ruki and Tilly ran off together. They're probably going to kiss or something. I think it's been obvious to everyone but Ruki that they're in love. I hope Tilly finally tells her. I've been dying to tease her about it ever since we met Tilly, but I knew it'd be more romantic if she figured it out on her own. I'm a sucker for good romance, it always makes a great story.

I figured while everyone else was busy, Gintina and I should look around this place. If it was going to be her new home, she was going to have to meet her new roommates. Our first stop was a large green space surrounded by a fence. A beautiful white horse walked up to greet us. I didn't know horses were magical, but what do I know? I walked up to the edge of the fence and held my palm out for the horse to approach on their own. This was something I'd seen the Goblin herders in my tribe do.

The horse walked up to me and lowered its head to me. Success! I slowly approached its head with my hand and began scratching. I felt something rough beneath my hand, so I shifted my scritches in a way that moved its mane off the area. I saw what looked like a jagged bone in the middle of its head. That made more sense. This must be a unicorn with a broken horn. I know those are magical!

I held up both hands so the unicorn could see I wasn't doing anything threatening and I climbed over the fence. I snapped my fingers over my shoulder to signal Gintina to raise up.

"Gintina, this is, well, this is embarrassing. I never got your name. Do you want me to just make one up for now?" I asked the unicorn. It shook its head. "Well, this is a unicorn that you will learn the name of later. It seems very nice, why don't you say hi?"

Gintina began to slink up my arm and slowly approached the unicorn. Gintina tilted her head when she reached the end of my arm and shyly flapped her wings. The unicorn looked cautious, but didn't make any sudden moves. That was probably good enough.

"You can get back in the bag now, Gintina. That was real good." I directed my attention back at the unicorn. "Do you want to show us around? We'd be really grateful."

The unicorn knelt down and offered its back to us. This was exciting! I hadn't ridden a horse, or a horse-like creature, since I was a teenager! I climbed onto its back and let it take the lead. It circled around the yard and ran towards the fence. It took a big leap and made it to the other side of the fence. This didn't feel like something I was supposed to do, but hey, I'm an adventurer. The rules don't apply to me.

The unicorn galloped along the edge of the fence until we reached a pond that was half inside the corral, half outside the corral. The horse let out a loud neigh. I think it was trying to tell someone something, but I had no idea if Gintina and I were the someones. It didn't take long to realize that it was something else. The water erupted, and we were showered with it. Gintina poked her head up from the bag to see what was going on. Another horse-like creature emerged from the pond. This one only really looked like a horse in its shape. If I weren't this close to it, I would probably think it was some kind of fish. It was green, covered in scales, and it had a blowhole on its head, like a dolphin. It cocked its head at us, and the unicorn knelt, putting Gintina and me at eye level with the sea-horse-thing.

"Hi! I'm Gin, and this is my friend, Gintina," I said, gesturing to the gwiber in my backpack. Gintina rested her head on my shoulder and rolled around on her back. I was pretty sure it was meant as some kind of greeting. "She's going to be moving here pretty soon, and I thought it'd be a good idea for her to meet everyone. Our unicorn friend here was showing us around. Do you have a name?"

The sea-horse thing lowered its head in a sort of nod.

"I figured. But you probably can't tell us, right? That makes sense. Well, it's nice to meet you. Is there anyone else in the water we should meet?"

It dove back into the pond, and the unicorn ran around to the other side of the pond. I didn't know if the unicorn was taking us somewhere else or if the sea-horse was getting someone else for us to meet. Before too long, the sea-horse poked its head back up, and a terrifying fish-cat kinda thing crawled out of the water. The unicorn made little circles with its head, probably in response to my sudden jump when I saw the cat thing. Its face was like any mountain lion I'd seen in the jungle, except it was bright blue. It also had paws and claws like a large cat, but its torso was much longer, almost like a serpent. There were shiny brown horns, the color of copper, poking out of its head. It opened its mouth to show its fangs. Even I knew this creature wanted to attack us. The sea-horse thing must have seen the fear in my eyes and swam around to the other side of it and splashed it with water. The water cat looked around and crept back into the water, like it forgot we were there.

"Remember that the water cat thing is pretty grumpy. I don't want you getting hurt," I advised Gintina.

The unicorn nodded in the direction of the sea-horse, and it nodded in response. The unicorn spun around and started galloping in a different direction. I turned around to wave at the sea horse thing.

"Bye! I'm sure Gintina will be seeing much more of you!"

The unicorn arrived at a wooded area. I could hear whistling above us. The trees were probably full of different kinds of magical birds. The unicorn knelt down again, probably suggesting we climb down. I obliged and wandered into the forest. Once I passed the first couple of trees, I saw that this was filled with way more than just birds. There were all kinds of winged creatures. I saw a winged lion that was missing claws pacing around a clearing. I saw small bunnies with large antlers hopping around. I even saw a couple of gwibers flitting around above us between branches.

"This must really be your new home, Gintina!" I exclaimed. Gintina wrapped herself around my neck like a scarf. I noticed that she did this when she was scared.

"I know. I'll miss you too, girl. But this is for the best. You should be with other animals like you!"

She buried her head under herself, trying not to face her reality. I recognized it because I used to do it all the time in the jungle.

"I know it's hard. Change is always hard. But look at Tilly! She thought she was really happy secretly taking care of you in that cave. But she is like a totally different person around Karuk."

Gintina lifted her head and looked me in the eyes. I think she was starting to understand.

"You'll love it here! You just have to get used to it."

She began to loosen herself from around my neck, but she still didn't move towards the treetops.

"I had a feeling someone was here. It's not like Trixie to jump out of the corral," an elderly-sounding voice emerged from behind us.

I turned to see it belonged to an old man that was some sort of person I'd never seen before. He looked kind of like if a bat turned into a person but still had some features like a bat. He had pointy ears on the sides of his head and an upturned nose. He also had leathery-looking wings connecting his arms to his back.

"Hi! I'm Gin. I don't think I've ever met anyone like you before. Is it rude to ask?"

"Of course not. If anything is true here on the reserve, it's that you should always ask about something you don't understand," the old man said kindly. "My name is Gael and I'm a Roedor. There's people like me all over Reyes, but what we don't often see are Goblins. You must have come with that group that Reggie brought in."

"I did! We brought my little buddy, Gintina, to find a place where she can be safe." I gestured to the winged snake around my neck.

"Oh, I've never seen a gwiber so attached to someone before. You must be great with animals. You wouldn't be looking for a job, would you? The reserve could always use more folks with an affinity."

"Sorry, me and my friends are adventurers. I never really thought of myself as good with animals, but I had an awful lot of fun playing my music for Gintina."

"That must be it! When gwiber get a little older than your Gintina here, they make songs with their wings. You probably reminded her of her mother."

I liked the sound of someone appreciating my music. Gintina was my first dedicated fan! I was going to miss her. "I'm glad I could give her some comfort on our journey. Can you help me get her to join the other gwibers up there? She's not wanting to leave me."

"Why don't you play some of your music? It might get the others to come down and join her."

I smiled and swung my drum around. I started beating out one of my favorite rhythms, and Gintina floated in front of me and started moving around like she was dancing. The other gwibers glided down from the trees and began dancing with her. It made me happy to see her making friends. As I finished playing, all of the gwibers, including Gintina, drifted up to the branches.

"That is mighty impressive, son," the old man told me.

"It's what I do," I answered.

"Well, you're very talented. If you ever get tired of adventuring, come back here."

I considered the way I felt right now. I felt really good that we were able to find Gintina a home where she could grow up with other gwibers like her. She was going to live a better life because we risked our lives to get her here. This must be how adventurers feel all the time!

I smiled back at the old man. "I'm pretty sure I'm meant to be an adventurer."

There are Elves Here?

Before we left the magic animal reserve, Reggie mentioned something about there being a portal to the Fey Realm in the adjacent island nation of Kapoor. We'd all heard the story about how oppressive and scary the Elves were. I'd heard all my life about the tragic history my Orc ancestors had suffered under them. But Gin, Dara, Tilly, and I were adventurers now, and we wanted to see something if it sounded interesting. Traveling to a different world sounded like something adventurers should do. We decided that since we didn't have anything pulling us in any specific direction, traveling to Kapoor in order to travel through the Fey Gate would be a pretty good next adventure.

We traveled to the port town of Manos and bought tickets for a ship headed to Kapoor. We used a bit of the money we'd gotten from the King of Valnan to pay for it. It felt really weird to be able to just pay for convenience. Before I realized we had money, I was preparing to craft another boat out of whatever we could find. It was a relief to be able to let someone else worry about navigating the ship while we traveled.

The ship docked in the city of Dhanri. I thought my tribe worked hard, but they had nothing on the people of Kapoor. I couldn't believe how fast they were unloading the ships. After disembarking, I was further shocked at the crowded streets. I had been to Anglachel a few times with the hunting party before, and Anglachel is a massive city, but I think that because there is so much of it, the streets never got this full. Everyone was moving with purpose. Everyone except the four of us. We had no idea where we were going.

"Where we headed, Dara?" Gin asked, looking up at Dara expectantly.

I noticed our group was starting to get its own rhythm. It was kind of comforting to have a sense of how we'd interact with each other, like a family.

"We've only just gotten here, Gin," Dara began. "I know about as much about this place as you do."

"I doubt that," Tilly said under her breath.

"There are Elves here?" I asked, surprised. I had never met an Elf before, but the streets were swarming with them. It was full of a mix of dark-skinned Elves and Humans. I didn't know if I should be terrified or curious.

"Well, yeah," Dara answered. "The nation of Kapoor was founded when the River Elves traveled to the Human and Mascara nation of Tag. The Elves began to work with the Humans and eventually pushed the Mascara out."

"What do you know? I didn't know that," Gin commented.

"O.K., O.K.," Dara relented. "If we're looking for a gate to the Fey Realm, we probably want to start with some kind of church. I know the River Elves essentially forced their religion on Humans by co-opting elements of their native culture. Most people actually don't know that."

"Gods, we don't need a history lesson," Tilly complained.

"So we need to find a church," I repeated.

"I bet that guy could take us to one!" Gin exclaimed, pointing at a man pulling a cart loaded with seats for passengers.

Gin raced up to claim the cart, but not before a finely dressed Elf sat in it before he could get there. It took us a few tries to actually get one, but finally, a muscular Human that couldn't have been over 18 years old agreed to take us to the closest temple of Pro'Va in what he called a rickshaw. He only spoke a handful of North Elven words, so communication was challenging. He raced us through the streets of Dhanri at a perfect speed to take everything in. There were shops set up all along the street, not unlike the market district in Anglachel. What was different were the bright colors. Clearly, the stall owners knew they had to stand out if they wanted to compete here, and that they did. Stalls would have elaborate tapestries serving as awning and drapes in reds, blues, and yellows scattered throughout.

It didn't take long, with the various smells wafting from food vendors, to remember that it had been quite some time since we'd eaten a proper meal. Once the young man dropped us off at a tall, multi-level temple, we took a quick break to pick up some street food. An older Human man was manning a stall beside the temple. He had two giant pots on either side of him. He also didn't speak much of the common language, but he did understand once we showed him a few pieces of gold. He scooped out some orange rice from one pot and an assortment of meat and vegetables, with a similar orange hue, into a magically created bowl. This is similar to the street food in Anglachel. You had to eat it within an hour, or the food would spill everywhere when the bowl disappeared. One bowl looked like enough food for all four of us. We gave him three pieces of gold and sat down on the curb of the street.

Gin was the first to grab a bit of it, and immediately regretted it.

"Ahhhhh!" He wailed. "Hot, hot, hot, hot. . . .!"

He wasn't stopping until someone helped him. Dara pulled out a stone he'd collected from a river in The Jungle and chanted the word "Riwante." He raised his hand that wasn't holding the rock over Gin's mouth, and water poured out of it. Gin drank and began to calm down.

"It is really spicy, guys," Gin finally said.

"I think we figured that out already," Tilly teased.

We all tentatively dug in, and it was incredibly spicy. The food I ate growing up often contained chilies, but it did not have this level of heat. However, once we got past the heat, the flavors were rich and something totally unique. We eventually finished all of the meal and sat the soon-to-be disappearing bowl on the curb before heading into the temple.

The temple itself was made of stone and shaped like a pyramid. It was as tall as some of the tallest trees in The Jungle. We walked through the door and were blown away. It was beautiful. There was a tiled floor creating an interwoven intricate pattern. There were clear pillars carved from some sort of crystal. It looked magical. An Elven clergymanwearing a long, draping orange robe, approached us and began speaking in the same language everyone else had been using. He must have been able to tell from the looks on our faces that we didn't understand. He lifted his hand and pointed one finger to the sky, and performed a circular motion.

"Karana," he said. "Now, that's better. You can understand me now, yes?"

"Yes, we can!" Dara exclaimed. "That was a translation spell, and you did it like it was nothing. You must be really skilled!"

"I simply channel the essence of Pro'Va, the god of the natural world," he said.

"Father, I had heard of a god named Kawma," I said. "I was told he was the god of nature. Is there more than one?"

"Child, the domains of the gods are not as clear cut as everyone thinks," he advised. "But yes, the god you know as Kawma is one and the same as Pro'Va. Different lands have different names for the divine. And I am no priest. Here my parishioners call me swami. Why are you here?"

"We want to travel to the Fey Realm! We heard there was a gate here," Gin answered.

"Ahh, so you are pilgrims," the swami said.

"Yeah! That's it!" Gin quickly replied before any of us could contradict him.

"That explains your interesting collection of people. It is truly rare to see an Orc and a Goblin here," he said.

"We just love Kawma so much! We want to honor him," Gin lied convincingly.

"It is an honor to welcome you. I have tools for you," the swami said.

He supplied us with a map and gave each of us something he referred to as a sacred seed. Apparently, it is traditional for pilgrims of Pro'Va to plant these seeds on the other side of the portal. It sounds to me like an excuse for members of the church to do work for the River Elves.

With the map, the portal wasn't actually that hard to find. I took the lead, and Dara helped to figure out anything I couldn't. Eventually, we made it to a river that was marked on the map as the River Sayanna. All that was left to do was follow the river upstream. It started in the city and moved into a much more open green space. We could see houses in the distance that clearly indicated the rural part of Kapoor. Eventually, the river lead us to an outcropping of trees. These trees looked harder, sturdier than the trees I was familiar with in The Jungle. I was used to seeing the ground covered in vines and various flowers, this was all green grass. As we walked into the forested area, it was subtle at first, but became clear that all of the plant life was becoming progressively more dead. We saw a grouping of black husks of trees that grew together in an arch shape.

"I think that was the gate," Dara said.

"This doesn't feel right," I said. "Everyone stay on guard. I don't know what is going on here."

"I don't know if whatever caused this is still here," Tilly said. "Listen, this place is as quiet as a graveyard. And kinda looks like one, too."

"It could be something spiritual, but I don't sense any presence here other than us," Dara observed.

"So I guess we're not going to the Fey Realm," Gin sighed.

"Is there anything we could do?" I asked Dara.

Dara squinted in thought. "Maybe. At Arcana University, I read about this spell that could transfer life from one creature to another. It was something used by really dark wizards to steal life from children and stuff. But maybe we can use it here."

"You're not giving my life to these trees," Gin said. "I don't care how cool the Fey Realm is."

"No, I think we are carrying children," Dara said.

"The seeds!" I realized.

Dara nodded. "Yes, I think I might be able to transfer the potential life of the seeds into the trees that form the archway."

"So what do we do?" Gin inquired.

"Just give me your seeds and some time," Dara said.

Dara spent the next hour drawing an intricate magic circle in the dirt in front of the archway. He then drew a diamond design over top of the entire circle. He placed one seed at each point on the diamond. He then carefully walked into the center of the circle and took a deep breath.

"You've got this!" Gin encouraged.

"I hope so." Dara shrugged. "I've never tried to channel anything this powerful before."

"We're here if you need us," I reminded him. "We'll rush in if it looks like things are going bad."

"Thanks, that actually helps," Dara said. "O.K., everybody ready? I'm not entirely sure how this will play out."

"C'mon, Dara, you're a bleedin' genius," Tilly said.

Dara extended his arms out on either side of his body, and his hands began to glow with a sickly green light. Then he started to chant.

"Reseverne Forcineri Consumé. Reseverne Forcineri Consumé. Reseverne Forcineri Consumé!" He finished by raising his voice to a shout and slamming his hands onto the ground below. The green color extended from his hands and touched each of the seeds. The glow became brighter and brighter until it was hard to look at. Finally, the color raced back along the diamond shape back into Dara's hands. But this time, it wasn't just his hands that were glowing; it was his whole body. His face shifted to an expression of brief panic, then realization. He dashed to the archway and threw his hands in the middle, where the portal would be. The green drained from his body and seeped into the ground below. Color began to return to the trees that composed the arch. They began to regrow leaves and even bloom orange flowers. Dara stepped back, and the space between the arch began to shimmer and took on a silvery hue.

"You did it, Dara!" Gin exclaimed. "You saved the portal!"

"I did," he said, his voice indicating a hint of disbelief. His body began to sway and fall towards the ground, but not before I could run up and catch him.

"You O.K.?" I asked.

"Yeah, just a little tired. We should probably go through the portal now. I don't want to have to do that again," Dara suggested.

"We really doin' this?" Tilly asked.

"We are," I confirmed. "We're adventurers."

Can You Believe We're Going to Save the World?!?

I had never walked through a portal before. When I was really young, the Hukawan tribe had an incredibly old shaman that could use spatial magic. He would use it to visit other tribes deeper into the jungle. So I know that there are people that can use spatial magic to teleport and create portals, but I was never sure what really happened when you walked through it. Was it really you that passed through to the other side, or a magical copy? How would we even know? I knew that I basically accepted that none of those concerns mattered when I ran off with Gin and Dara to become an adventurer. Using magic to travel is just part of the gig.

I didn't know what to expect the Fey Realm to look like, but I definitely did not expect it to remind me so much of home. The ground was covered with plant life, and we were surrounded by trees, except for a humble dirt path leading deeper into the forest. I wasn't really sure what to do next. Were we just looking around? Now that we've done it, are we pretty much done now? I looked to Dara so I could follow his lead.

Dara was still stumbling, but began shambling forward down the path. I followed him without looking back because I knew Gin and Tilly would be close behind. I still didn't know where we were going, but I didn't have to wonder for long. The clearing opened up into a large settlement nestled in the trees. As soon as we emerged from the forest, an older Elven woman with dark skin ran up to us.

"Do you have word of the other side? What is happening?"

"We came here as part of a pilgrimage," I said, continuing our cover.

Her face told us that she was very worried. "We haven't seen anyone from the other side in weeks. We were worried something happened."

"You may be right about that," Dara began. "The portal gate wasn't working. All the trees and grass around it were dead. I was able to bring it back to life with my magic, but I don't know what caused it."

"He's trying to cross to the other side," she said cryptically.

"Who is he?" Tilly asked.

"As pilgrims, you must know that Pro'Va isn't truly the god the people of Kapoor worship. We all worship the Fey god, Sayanna. Sweet Sayanna was the one who granted Elves our great magic power. The seasonal courts forget, but we of the River remember," she said reverently.

"So this Sayanna is trying to come to Galevyn? That doesn't sound so bad. You just called her sweet," Gin concluded.

"Oh, were it just Sayanna I was referring to! You see, her brother, Puché has always been jealous of her. We should have seen this coming. Once we convinced the Humans to perform rituals to honor Sayanna, of course Puché would desire to cross over and destroy your world."

"Destroy? I don't like the sound of that," Tilly said.

"Nor should you," the Elven woman agreed. "We of the River have built a life utilizing both sides of the portal. It would be challenging to return to only utilizing our limited space in the Fey Realm."

"I'm sorry, who are you?" Dara said, a little frazzled. "This is a lot to take in. I've always learned there were eight gods. Every child in Anglachel knows that. And each god rules over a different domain of magic. That's just how it works. And you're telling me that Kawma was a different god all along?"

"Forgive me, young ones, my name is Sitara. I am the elder on this side of the gate." she said, introducing herself. "I do not know of this Kawma you speak of. We simply convinced the Humans of Kapoor to honor their god, Pro'Va, with rituals meant for our Sayanna. I do not know if Pro'Va or this Kawma you mention is real. I have my doubts based on what we know about the knowledge of those on your side of the gate. But Sayanna and Puché are both very real. Sayanna has continued to support us in your realm, now it appears Puché hopes to oppose us."

Well, that explanation was a mixed bag. I'm sure Dara was following it, but all I got was she called everyone from Galevyn stupid and thinks our gods are fake. But if there is a real threat against our home, someone had to do something. And are we adventurers, or are we adventurers?

"We have to help. What can we do?" I asked.

"Come with me. I have the supplies you will need to defeat Puché. He is likely posing as another god, much like our arrangement with Sayanna. However, his dark machinations are not meant for mainstream consumption. He likely has far fewer followers or at least many smaller sects. One of these must be gaining power. I imagine they would appear to you as an extremist cult to one of your world's other gods," she finished.

"Do you have any idea where we would even start?" Tilly said as we began to follow her.

"This I do know. Once the portal stopped functioning, I scryed on your world to see if there were any large collections of magic that would be associated with Puché. I found a heavy concentration of necromancy on the northeastern coast of the land your people refer to as Daragon," she said.

"Necromancy?" Dara said thoughtfully. "They must be posing as a Quietus cult."

"At least we're close to Daragon. I'm sorry, but does no one else feel really excited? Can you believe we're going to save the world?" Gin stated.

"I sure hope so, Gin," I replied.

Trust Me. I'm Weird.

Dara

How long does this friggin' desert go on for?" Gin grumbled.

His smallgoblin body was not used to the dry heat of Daragon. I was happy to be here. We'd already journeyed through the jungles of Anglachel, the mountains of Ferreira, and the marshlands of Kapoor. The deserts of Daragon was one of the last two distinct geographic regions of Galevyn I had to check off my bucket list. We were so close to being able to say we'd literally traveled across the planet.

"We should be there any minute now," Karuk reassured him.

"You told him that an hour ago," Tilly reminded her. "Are you sure you're reading that map right?"

"I know what I'm doing," Karuk insisted.

"I trust her," I said.

"Why don't you make sure, Dara," Gin whispered loud enough for Karuk to hear.

"Yeah, you could make sense of this complex geography," Tilly commented sarcastically, gesturing to the miles of desert around us.

I hated being the smart one. I trusted Karuk's instincts. She knew how to guide us through Hell itself. I could trust her to get us through a desert. I didn't like being the one my companions relied on to check her work.

I walked up to her and took a look at her map. As far as I could tell, the map matched up to the place that we currently were. I mean, a blank desert looks like a blank desert, whether it is in person or on a map.

"We seem to be on the right track," I reassured them.

The sighs from Tilly and Gin were audible. What could I tell them? Walking through a desert is boring. It is big and it takes a while to get through. I don't know what they expected. Karuk turned her head towards me and gave me an approving smile, her Orc tusks creeping over her mouth. I gave her a knowing nod and settled back to my spot into the middle of our party.

"I hope the lead we got from that old woman was right. I'd hate to be sweating through my favorite pair of travel pants for nothing," Gin complained.

"What an intriguing thought," Tilly snapped. "I'm certain no one else among us has had a similar thought."

"I'm just trying to keep my mind off this heat," Gin explained. "Let's talk about something. What do you got, Dara?"

"What?" I asked, surprised.

"Come on, buddy. You're always wanting to talk about your magic stuff. This is your chance. You've got a fully captive audience," Gin suggested. Tilly let out a choked laugh.

I didn't know where he was getting this. I wasn't going around trying to talk to them about my magic. I was just always thinking about magic and sometimes my thoughts found their way out of my mouth. I'd always presumed they understood that. Then again, I don't think that ever escaped my thoughts.

"Do you really want to hear about the nuanced differences of fire and lava magic?" I asked, hoping the idea of it would bore him into accepting silence.

"Please, no heat talk," Gin pleaded. "Maybe you can talk about, like, ice and water magic. Is that a thing? Maybe the thought of it would cool us off."

"I can see your thought process, but it is very different. Ice and water magic are actually both water magic," I said.

"Great!" Gin said, "Keep going. That works for me."

"I don't know if the magic talk will keep me entertained," Tilly spoke up from our flank, "but the show the two of you are putting on is pretty great."

Karuk laughed from up front.

"Now, you need to keep paying attention to where we're going," Tilly chastised.

"Tilly, you know I could do this in my sleep," Karuk reassured her. "We just have to keep going northwest until we run into a savannah."

"Right! The famous Savannah of the Dragon. I don't know how I could have forgotten it," I exclaimed.

"What are you going on about now?" Gin asked.

"That blasted list of his," Tilly said. "He wants to travel to all the interesting places in Galevyn."

"Did I know that?" Gin said.

"Probably not," Karuk said. "You're always too busy listening to yourself talk to hear anybody else."

"Did you say something, Karuk?" Gin asked.Gin let out his mischievous giggle, while Karuk chucked a pebble over her shoulder and hit Gin squarely in the head."Hey Karuk!" he chided. "Where did you even get a pebble? It's been desert and sand ever since we got to Daragon."

"I hung onto one from Kapoor," Karuk said matter-of-factly.

Gin shook his head. "You're so weird."

"Hey, that's my girlfriend," Tilly playfully snapped.

"That doesn't mean she's not weird. If anything it probably makes her more weird. An Orc dating a Gnome? Come on, it is a little weird," Gin said.

"Says the singing Goblin," Karuk retorted.

"Sure. We're all weird," Gin said. "No one is denying that. I was just commenting on your specific brand of weirdness."

"It's why we work together," I suggested.

"You're not that weird," Tilly commented. "You're just a Human who studied magic. The weirdest thing about you is that you chose to hang out with us."

"Trust me, I'm weird," I assured them. "I'm a Human that dropped out of Arcana University because he thought he was smarter than the teacher. I'm a Human who always talks to himself but has trouble talking to other people."

Gin considered this. "That's just socially awkward."

"Welcome to weird for Humans!" I exclaimed. "Trust me, I was the guy in school that everyone pointed at and said 'That guy's weird!'"

"Humans are the worst," Tilly said. "Present company excluded."

"You'll hear no arguments from me," I agreed.

"Look alive, folks," Karuk barked from up front. "Monster ahead."

"What are we looking at?" Tilly asked.

Gin looked all around. "I don't see anything."

"It just went underground. There's a sand wyrm ahead, I think it's headed our way," Karuk explained.

I combed through my brain to figure out what would work well against a sand wyrm. It attacks its prey by pulling them underground. That's it! I pulled out my spell component pouch and grabbed a crystal and began twirling it between my fingers.

"Alright guys, get ready to jump. Things might get a little chilly," I warned.

Gin pumped his fist into the air. "Sweet!"

I channeled my magic energy into the crystal until I could see it leave small bits of frost as it twirled. I slammed my hand into the sand and said the magic words. "Iceslo Comformum!" I screamed.

My companions jumped into the air as a thick sheet of ice began to cover the sand below us. I quickly pulled my hand away before it could get frozen in place. Just as my spell finished, we heard a loud thump. Fissures began to form in the middle of the ice disc I'd just created.

"I coulda done that," Gin jested.

Tilly gave Gin a stink eye. "Shut up."

There was blood starting to show below the ice. We could also see the monster's teeth as it worked on chewing through the surface. Gin and I walked to the edge of the disc, and Tilly crouched down in front of us, getting ready to pounce. Meanwhile, Karuk drew her hand ax and stood ready by the creature's head. Gin began to pound out a rhythm on his drum and thin magical barriers began to form around each of our forms. I began digging through my component pouch, preparing my next spell. This wasn't our first fight.

Once we each got into position, the wyrm crashed out of the icy surface. Karuk slammed down onto it with her ax. Brown wyrm blood splashed up and coated her cloak. Tilly ran up to flank the beast and dug both of her daggers into the back of its head. The creature wailed in pain, but it wasn't finished yet.

It managed to push half of its body out of the hold and crunched down on Karuk. The kind of pressure it caused would normally kill an Orc of Karuk's size, but Gin's barrier magic held strong. The spell I wanted to cast called for glass shards, but I didn't have any in my component pouch. I looked around and realized there were basically tiny shards of glass all around us. I turned around and scooped up a handful of sand. I began chanting as I rushed up to the wyrm. "Frosto Consumae, Frosto Consumae, Frosto Consumae."

I plunged my hand into the open wound Karuk's ax had created and released the sand. Frost began to spread throughout the creature's body. Its eyes began to freeze over as its life came to an end.

I went over and pulled Karuk down from the dead wyrm's mouth.

"You o.k.?" I asked.

"Yeah, great. I feel exhilarated!" she exclaimed.

"I've never seen that spell before," Tilly said. "Is that new?"

"A little," I said. "I just adapted an ice attack spell to create an aura and . . ."

"Please don't go on again," Gin said.

We all laughed. Karuk sliced off a chunk of the creature and built a fire to turn it into jerky. I cast a fire spell to dispose of the rest of the corpse. After a short break, we continued our journey.

"How much longer, Karuk?" Gin asked.

"We should reach the savannah any minute now," she replied.

"I swear you said the same thing an hour ago," Tilly complained.

I smiled to myself and started thinking about what we'd find at the Savannah of the Dragon. I was going to have to start a new list.

Acknowledgments

This book came together because I got tired of editing my first novel and wanted to start writing again. I didn't want to write a sequel to the novel, because I hadn't plotted out the potential series yet. I decided I would write short stories about side characters, or characters tangentially connected to the main characters in the novel. I ended up using these stories as a way to flesh out and fully build the fantasy world of Galevyn. Along the way, I fell in love with Asha, Karuk, and Rowena (and Gin, he's a blast to write).

That's how this book came together. But I never could have done it without the help and encouragement of a lot of incredible people.

The first person I have to thank is my best friend, Dustin Whitman. He has been my biggest cheerleader and has been keeping me accountable every step of the way. We've been jokingly referring to him as my agent, but I think that somewhere along the way it might have actually happened.

I also need to give a giant thank you to my brother, Allen Bartley. I have literally bounced literally every idea, character, plot point, and storyline off of him. He probably isn't reading this because I'm sure he's tired of hearing about these characters by now and he could probably recite every story in here.

I'd like to thank my writing buddies and grammar friends, Robb Livingood, Heather Pettry, Brandie Newsom, Angela Jones, and Heather Hayes. You all helped make me look good and also talk through every weird fantasy grammar question I had.

Thank you to Deryl Arrazaq for creating the incredible cover. My editor Erin Bledsoe, thank you for helping me get some perspective on my characters and making sure readers know every setting isn't a white void. Bethany Atazadeh, I don't know you, but your Youtube videos gave me the confidence to put all this together. Thank you to Ariel Price and Mike Pereira for your design advice. My writing colleagues and mentors, Sam J. Miller, Cody Walker, Kirsha Fox, Andrea Fink, and Amada Ross, thank you for all your advice and for making me feel like I'm part of a larger community. To the band, Sub-Radio, thank you for your constant inspiration.

Finally, thank you to Sandra Bartley, Betty Oquendo, Audrey Sands, Sara Price, Jeff McNeely, Mackenzie Price, Dan Taylor, Chase Henderson, Rachel Henderson, Eric Hager, AJ Smith, and Melinda Piccirillo for helping me feel like I could do this and for all of the intangible ways you helped me throughout this process. I'm sure there are people I left out and for that I'm sorry and please know that I appreciate you too!

Preview:

I'm an Expert Assassin and I Don't Even Get a Name?!?

Coming Spring 2024

I woke up in my non-descript slate room as I had every other day for all 18 years of my life. I slumped my legs off of my stone bed and sat up. I looked down at my grey legs and noticed that my carapace looked like it had grown a bit harder. Maybe I really was growing up. I had spent so long as a changeling youth that it hardly seemed possible. But today was the day I would get my first job from The Sovereign.

It felt strange to be getting a job by myself. My entire life I hadn't thought much about myself as an individual. After a changeling baby is born, they are immediately placed in the nursery. There every child is treated as a collective unit. Every changeling is the same, we are all part of the collective. Even during our training, we are all taught to perform at the peak level expected of us. Creative thought is discouraged. Missions must be completed in a very specific way and none of us are allowed to stray from the method.

Tyranny of the Fey

You may be wondering what kind of missions we do. You would be forgiven if you had never heard of the Changeling Collective before. There was a time when the collective was a major player in Galvyn politics, but The Collective learned that we are better served operating in the shadows. We provide an important service to the people of Galvyn. We keep power in check. We are assassins.

I left my room and walked down the long hallway. Every changeling is housed in this large dormitory. The only reason we are given our own space once we come of age is to become accustomed to living on our own. It is important that we are able to function independently when we are on our missions. We need to be able to fully become our cover identity.

Once I reached the end of the hallway, I started heading to the throne room of The Sovereign. The skies above were the same grey as my carapace. This was a good sign. The Sovereign is only known through their title. Whenever The Sovereign dies, a new Sovereign is chosen from the oldest changeling operatives. They are not considered better than us, The Collective simply requires a leader and The Sovereign serves that function.

Once I reached the gates of The Sovereign throne room, I presented myself to the guards.

"I am here to receive my first assignment," I explained to the guards.

"What is your name?" The guard asked.

"I have no name. I am of The Collective. We are The Collective," I recited from my training.

"We are the collective," the guard said, pushing the gate open behind him.

"You may proceed."

The throne room was as I had learned it would look in my training. The ceilings were higher than any I had ever seen. The room was the same grey slate that I had become accustomed to, but the path to the throne was lined with pillars on either side. Elaborate carvings of daggers, crossbows and poison vials, traditional changeling weaponry, adorned the pillars. The Sovereign sat upon their throne at the end of the walkway. They wore no jewelry or fancy clothing. They were simply sitting upon the grey throne, naked as any other changeling within the walls of Aristogen. The Sovereign truly was no different than the rest of us.

"What brings you here, child," The Sovereign asked as I reached the base of the throne. I knelt down to show respect.

"I have come of age," I replied. "I am here to accept my first mission."

"Stand, child, you owe me no more respect than you owe any other of The Collective," The Sovereign commanded. I stood up.

"Of course, Sovereign," I replied.

"From this day forth, you will be given Designation 27. If you would allow me a moment of sentimentality, that was my number when I was an operative. It is a pleasure to meet my successor," The Sovereign stated.

This startled me. Changelings were not meant to feel attached to any identity. It seemed as though The Sovereign was giving me permission to form a personal identity around my designation. This was a more exciting day than I realized. I tried not to let the emotion show on my face.

"It is an honor to serve in this position," I commented.

"It is not," The Sovereign stated. "Serving is a part of life for members of the collective. But I do understand the intent behind your words and I do appreciate them."

The Sovereign stood up and picked up a leather satchel from a table beside the throne. They walked down and handed it to me.

"This is your assignment dossier," The Sovereign explained. "Study it. This will be everything you need to know about your identity for this job and what needs to be accomplished."

"I will," I assured them. "Is there anything else I need to know?"

"There is not. A changeling operative is never curious. They only follow orders," The Sovereign reminded me.

"We are the collective," I replied.

"We are the collective," The Sovereign repeated. "Now go back to your room and study your dossier. Head to the docks at first light tomorrow as your new identity. You have been trained for this. You will know what to do."

I bowed my head slightly and turned to leave. I did not look back, because I knew The Sovereign would not want me to think of anything other than the mission ahead of me. Although, I had trouble not thinking about my new identity. I am part of the collective, but I am also Designation 27. I have a name.

About the Author

Terry Bartley is a journalism, literature, and English teacher at Scott High School. Terry is the host of the podcast "Most Writers are Fans," about the intersection between writing and fandom. Terry has professionally written for the Coal Valley News and Screenrant. He has won awards for writing and broadcasting from the West Virginia Associated Press, the National Broadcasting Society, and MarCom. He has a B.A. in English from the University of Phoenix and an M.A. in English Education from Western Governor's University. He loves tabletop roleplaying games, social deduction games, reading comics, and watching musical television shows. He lives in rural West Virginia with his dog, Etsy.

Thanks for reading "Tyranny of the Fey." I'd really appreciate it if you could write a review on Amazon or Goodreads. It really helps out indie authors. Check out merch based on this book, read other stories set in the Galevyn universe, sign up for my newsletter, and see my upcoming media and public appearances on my website, terrybartley.com. Finally, follow me on social media to see my thoughts on nerdy things or watch my fantasy-themed parody music videos.

Twitter: *@terrybartley*

TikTok: *@terrlet*

Instagram: *@terrlet*

Facebook: *@terrybartleywriter*

Discord: *bit.ly/byterrybartley-discord*

Podcast: *Most Writers Are Fans*